CHRONICLES ABROAD

Istanbul

CHRONICLES ABROAD

Istanbul

CHRONICLE BOOKS
SAN FRANCISCO

CHRONICLES ABROAD

Istanbul

Printed in Singapore.

Page 190 constitutes a continuation of the copyright page.

Library of Congress Cataloging-in-Publication Data:

Istanbul / edited by John and Kirsten Miller.

p.   cm. — (Chronicles Abroad)

ISBN 0-8118-0823-8

1. Istanbul (Turkey)—Miscellanea. 2. Istanbul (Turkey)—Literary collections.

I. Miller, John, 1959-   . II. Miller, Kirsten, 1962-

III. Series.

DR719.I73   1995

949.61'8—dc20   94-34514

CIP

Editing and design: Big Fish Books
Composition: Jennifer Petersen, Big Fish Books

Distributed in Canada by Raincoast Books,
8680 Cambie Street, Vancouver, B.C. V6P 6M9

10 9 8 7 6 5 4 3 2 1

Chronicle Books
275 Fifth Street
San Francisco, CA 94103

Contents

Joseph Brodsky

THERE ARE PLACES where history is inescapable,
like a highway accident—places whose geography pro-
vokes history. Such is Istanbul, alias Constantinople, alias
Byzantium. A traffic light gone haywire, with all three colors flaring up at once. Not red-amber-green but white-
amber-brown. Also, of course, blue: for the water, for the
Bosporus-Marmara Dardanelles, which separates Europe

Russian poet and critic Joseph Brodsky is best known for his collections, A
Part of a Speech *and* Less Than One, *which won the Pulitzer Prize in
1987. This excerpt is from his 1985 paean to Istanbul, "Flight from Byzantium." It originally appeared in the* New Yorker.

from Asia—or does it? Ah, all these natural frontiers, these straits and Urals of ours! How little they have ever meant to armies or cultures, and even less to non-cultures—though for nomads they may actually have signified a bit more than for princes inspired by the linear principle and justified in advance by an entrancing vision of the future.

Bahloal Dana

THE ROSE OF ISTAMBOUL

ONLY TWENTY-THREE, but already he had three wives. These had been thrust upon him by family and political exigencies. His first wife, Zara, was six years older than he, a cumbrous, over-sensible woman. Ayesha, the second, had been the young widow of a wealthy and childless pasha who had left her everything, and such a prize Seyd's mother could not resist for him. Danäe was a

---

Bahloal Dana's "The Rose of Istamboul" dates to the Ottoman empire. While the story is considered a classic of Turkish literature, little is known about its mysterious author.

Greek, a prisoner of the last rebellion, given him by his General as a reward. He could not refuse her, and his native chivalry denied any other arrangement save marriage.

He had wished for none of these women, all three had been thrust upon him. They were content enough, but although he was kind, considerate and friendly with all three, he cared for none of them. He cared only for the beauty of the spiritual. He told himself that he should have been a Sufi, one of those poet-priests whose hermit lives are given over to the ecstasy of the contemplation of the divine.

But this evening, as he stepped to his barge through the most beautiful garden on the banks of the Golden Horn, Seyd realized that hermitage was really unnecessary to ecstatic thinking and living. Here was Paradise at his very gate.

Through the white columns of the Byzantine ruins standing where the garden met the sea, glowed the island-bearing sapphire of the Bosphorus, a plane of light

beneath a turquoise sky dashed with thin gold. The linea-
ments on the marble capitals were clear as in the sculp-
tor's thought, and the stony wreaths of ivy, myrtle and
pine which clustered the shattered pillars seemed only not
to move and grow because no wind vexed the night's first
rapture. It was good to live not for vitality's sake, but for
the sake of that essence of the seraphic which drenches
the airs of that golden place.

The light barge, under the compelling hands of
its four negro rowers, thrust its nose towards the jutting
lands which almost meet at the bay's entrance. Seyd lit a
chibouque, and lay back in the cushions, taking in the
magic of the evening. A frail drift of opal cloud held the
upper sky, and the stars through this gazed as women's
eyes through veiling. Women's eyes! He smiled rather bit-
terly. To him there had always seemed more of devil than
angel in womankind. They were not serene, they had no
depths of mind or soul, they were prone to obsessions
and gross superstitions which cling to them like weed to

the body of a ship. They were spirits of impulse, hating and loving in a breath. Allah alone knew why He had created them. Foolish men were captured by their little coquetries, but wise men avoided the snare of them, as they avoided all that was not good for the soul's life.

The barge shot though the harbour's mouth and continued its course round the coastal fringe of silver sand lying without the Horn. The heaped miracle of Istamboul rose behind him, a mountain of minarets and rainbow domes, lofting into the illimitable turquoise of the Eastern night. At the spectacle of it, beautiful as a wreck of Paradise his eyes overflowed with tears. When Nature and Man set hands to the same canvas what, with the aid of Allah, could they not achieve?

The barge drew shoreward, and toward a small jetty. Seyd landed, and told the negroes to wait. He walked inland by a narrow path, plunging into a little wood where a small ruined mosque stood in deserted whiteness. Although it was roofless and long deserted, although the incense of prayer seldom ascended here, Seyd piously removed his peaked shoes before he entered. Some rainwater, limpid as aquamarine, lay in the shattered basin, and in this he made his ablutions.

Seating himself on one of the tilting flagstones, he began to pray, devoutly, utterly oblivious to all his surroundings. This indeed was life, this communion with the Merciful, the Compassionate, Sultan and Sovereign of the Universe, of the seas and the stars, of men and of angels. The power of the Divine interpenetrated every fibre of him, overflowing into his spirit in mystical golden rapture, making his heart blossom in love and the comprehension of heaven. He could understand how the Patriarchs and the Prophets who walked with God had endured material existence but for such moments as this, which brought a sense of the everlasting beauty and nobility of the bond betwixt God and man. This was indeed life, joy, victory!

A slight noise behind him disturbed his devotions. He turned his head. He rose quickly. Before him in the gathering shadows which fell like thick curtains upon the little mosque stood a woman heavily veiled. A sudden resentment seized him. To behold a woman there and at such an hour seemed monstrously inappropriate. Some crone, doubtless, who, with the privilege of age, came there to make secret devotions. Then he saw by her bare feet, white as alabaster, that she was a young woman. It was not meet that he should be there alone with her. He would go.

But as he made to do so, he found his way barred by a shapely arm.

"Stay, Seyd," she said in a deep rich voice that thrilled him to the deepest places of his blood. "Stay, for I am the answer to your prayer."

Amazed, he could scarcely speak. "How lady," he stammered. "I seem to know you, but. . . ." Then the truth of the matter rushed in upon him. This was some woman of love, some courtesan who had tracked him here, seeking to beguile him and bring him to shame, a ghoul, perhaps, sent by Eblis to destroy him, soul and body.

"Let me pass," he said sternly. Her answer was to raise her veil, and at the sight, Seyd gave back in amazed terror, for at once he knew that this was no mere mortal beauty, but a miraculous and elemental loveliness such as it is given only to the inspired and the saintly to behold.

"Who art thou?" he asked in great fear, his flesh shaking as though it would fall asunder and dissolve.

"Ask not my name, Seyd. Be content that I have been sent to thee in answer to thy unuttered prayers. Allah in His great mercy has understood that for thee and such as thee no mortal woman can suffice. But as it is necessary that the soul of woman should unite with that even of the most wise and pious of mankind, such as I have been raised up by Allah to attend them in order that the miracle of nature's unity may be made complete."

Seyd was silent for a long time. "Much of what you say is dark to me," he said at last. "It may be that in my dreams and even while in prayer I have sought the perfect woman, though I knew it not. But how am I to know whether you are of the divine or a demon from Eblis? Sheitan sends strange and beautiful shapes to decoy the holy from their allegiance to Allah."

The woman laughed. "Nay seek, not to number me among the devils," she said, "for were I a demon I might not utter the name of Allah. Nor might I enter this holy mosque, deserted as it is. And that I am more than woman, you have but to look at me to be convinced. Come, Seyd, reject me not, for it is the will of Allah that you should love and cherish me, of Allah who would have nothing single, who has sent love into the world for all men's worship and acceptance."

As she spoke, she drew near, and, holding out her arms, folded him in an embrace so full of warm life and rapture, that, intoxicated, he returned it with almost equal ardour. His senses reeled at her kisses, his mood of cold insensibility fell from him like a garment outworn. For the first time he experienced the overwhelming miracle of love. The hours passed with dreamlike rapidity in the little mosque. Seyd, the passionless, the chilly hearted, felt himself transported as if to the seventh heaven of delight. Profound as was the rapture of prayer, of communion with Allah, this was an experience more divine.

"You have not told me your name," he said, "but already I know it. For you are Mystery, whom all men love, but whose love few achieve while still in life."

"Mystery I am, as thou sayest, O Seyd," she replied. "Yet is that not all of me. I am something more, something you encounter every day, something you love well, and for which you would gladly give your life, yet which daily you tread under your feet."

"You are also Love, mayhap?"

"Yes. Love I am, Love the most profound, a love

surpassing that of the mother for the son, the sailor for the sea."

A thin light broke through the canopy of the darkness.

"It is the hour before dawn," whispered the woman, "we must part, Seyd, my beloved. But come to me here soon. I shall keep tryst here each nightfall in the hope of meeting thee."

And so they parted with a lingering kiss. Seyd quickly made his way back to the barge, to find that his four negroes had long fallen asleep. Awaking them, he was rowed speedily home. All night he dreamed of the woman he had met in the ruined mosque.

When he rose the next day, it was to be assailed with doubt. Surely she must be a thing of evil, a ghoul such as the peasants spoke of, haunting ruined mosques and graveyards, a lamia such as the old legends told of, seeking to lure men to destruction. Yet of evil in her he had seen not the least admixture. Her bearing, her speech were natural and unaffected. It was chiefly the comprehension of something elemental in her, some power indescribable, that nurtured his misgivings.

All that day he walked in his garden, deep in meditation. That his lady had entered a mosque showed at least that she was not a thing, an appearance, sent by the powers of Eblis for his destruction. Holy mullahs and imaums praying in the desert, had been beset by such, and through their influence, delivered over to the father of the night. There was, of course, no imaginable test by which he could know absolutely that she was a veritably a woman, unless he traced her to her dwelling-place. He recalled it as strange that when he had glanced back at the mosque when half-way to his barge that he had not seen her emerge from the only doorway the shrine had.

At nightfall after a troubled day, he ordered his caique once more, and was rowed to the little jetty. It was now almost quite dark, and as he entered the mosque, he saw a white shape bending to and fro in the actions of prayer. This dissolved his last fear that he had to deal with a creature unhallowed. Springing forward, he seized her in his arms, and was greeted with rapture.

"The day has been long," he said, "but its sorrows are over. I have thought of you through all the hours. I must know who you are—know your name."

"My name, beloved? Call me the Rose of Istamboul if though wilt, for indeed I have none other you may know."

"The Rose of Istamboul! Truly that is a fair name enough, sweet, and so I shall call you, for the present at least. But when you become my bride, then I must know your true name."

"Your bride, Seyd? Am I not already your bride? Think you that the mutterings of a few words by the imaum alone makes man and woman one?"

"But I am resolved that you shall dwell in my house, moon of my eyes," cried Seyd in agitation. "Nay it must be so."

"Let us forget the thoughts of men for the present," she replied, clinging to him. "Let us remember only the elemental things—the things which make up real existence."

And so the night passed as that before it had done, and night after night Seyd met the Rose of Istamboul. He might not put aside his longing that they should share existence wholly, by day as well as by night. He craved to see her in his house, to eat with her, to share the common things of life with her, and often did he tell her so. But to his pleadings she was silent. When he spoke thus, not a word did she answer.

At length he resolved to discover her identity, to find out where she lived. He had never, so far, seen her come or go at their rendezvous. So one night after leaving her in the little mosque as usual, he waited in the shadow of the trees which surrounded it, intent on following her.

Nearly half an hour passed, and he had almost resolved to retrace his steps to see whether she still remained in the mosque, when she passed the spot where he had concealed himself. Creeping stealthily from his hiding-place, he followed her. She walked slowly for some considerable distance over the rough bent which stretched between the seashore and the city. Suddenly, the first ray of daylight throbbed across the sapphire dusk of night. Distracted from his intention for an instant by the beauty of the sight, an arrow of silver flying across an azure shadow, he cast his glance upward, and when he brought it back to the point where she had last appeared it was to find no trace of her. She had vanished as completely as though she had dissolved into the vapours of the morning which now began to rise from the plains behind the sea.

In a frenzy he ran onward, calling her name. "Rose, Rose of Istamboul, where are you?" But nothing could he see except the level bent where sand lay at the roots of each tuft of coarse grass, nothing could he hear except the low wind of sunrise sighing across the waste.

Despondently, he returned to his barge, and was

rowed homeward. He had become aware that Zara, his chief wife, was suspicious of his nightly movements. Although she made no complaint, she frequently looked at him with deep reproach. As for the others, for days at a time he scarcely saw them. All three had become repugnant to him. To free himself from them was impossible.

Then he recalled that this woman who had taken him body and soul had told him that she was more than woman, that she was, indeed, the answer to his prayer—a prayer he had been unconscious of offering up. Of what folly had he not been capable? That, good or evil, the Rose of Istamboul was a creature of spiritual mould he was now assured. Her disappearance on the seashore in the twinkling of an eye proved as much. He must see her no more, he must content himself with life as he found it; as a true man should.

So no more he went to the mosque in the little wood. Days passed, and although grief gnawed at his heart as a serpent, he kept his own house at nights. His wife Zara was pleased with him, and even refrained tormenting the little Greek, Danäe, while the young but experienced Ayesha, who had been married before to an elderly roue, smiled secretly, and tittered when he went to the casement, opening it on the view of the Golden Horn.

But he could not harden his heart against the Rose of Istamboul, for the lure of her was such as it is not given to man to resist, the lure of earth, of air, of nature, of the deep indwelling life which lies in the soil's womb, in the bodies of trees, in the breath of life which we call the wind. All that the eye might see, all that the ear might hear, recalled the miracle of her, who was compounded of atoms and essences natural and delectable. The woods were her hair, the planets her eyes, the sea her spirit. And Seyd knew that she might not be escaped by any man, because, as she had said, she was not only woman, but all that woman in her essential native vigour and power and divine sweetness brings to man in one body—the rapturous spirit of that earth of which he is himself a part, the less vivid, the less daedal part, the nymphic fire that from the oak conceives the dryad, that from the stream brings forth the naiad, that pagan fury which not only receives the life of which man is the vessel, but which has power, like its mother the earth, to bring it to harvest and fruition.

Stunned for a space by the revelation of what he had lost, he leaped from his divan with the frenzy of a man who had cast away a whole world. His slaves shrank from him in terror as they beheld him. With speechless gestures he commanded them to prepare the caique. They obeyed and in a few moments he was cleaving the waters of the Golden Horn once more, the foam rising upon the prow, turning into snow the reflected heaven of Bosphorus.

And so he came to the little mosque and found her there. Once more he was enfolded in her arms, he drank of her loveliness.

"Ah," she cried, gazing into his eyes with rapture, "all is well at last. You know Seyd, you understand. For I am what comes to all poets, I am the soil as woman, as bride, she who at last arises out of the earth they love better than themselves to cherish them and be with them always. I am the Rose of Istamboul!"

Mary Lee Settle

THE LORDS AND LADIES OF BYZANTIUM

THE TURKISH THAT I speak is direct, like a child's. I call it, honoring *Casablanca,* "such much" Turkish. So this language, with its echoes of nomads and emperors, pashas and *ghazis,* sultans and riches, and country matters, with its verbs of more than forty tenses, including the very useful one for innuendo that I wish we had, its oblique politenesses, this language with its own poetry of front- and back-rhyming vowels, this old tongue that con-

Mary Lee Settle is the author of over a dozen novels, a memoir, and three collections of essays, including the critically acclaimed Turkish Reflections *(1991).*

tains within it all the past of Anatolia, is, for me, a short-hand. I get along, though. Turks are very polite people.

"*Korkuyorum,*" I said. I am scared.

He held up one imperious hand and stopped the traffic. To the music of furious horns, he took my hand and led me slowly across the street called the *Divan Yolu*— the road to the palace that followed the Roman Mese, the great central artery of old Constantinople, the Roman road the runs from the Hagia Sophia to the Theodosian walls and beyond, aimed straight at the heart of Europe. This was the road of the Janissaries, the Crusaders, the armies of Mehmet II, the Turkish conqueror of Istanbul.

We reached the other side. "*Çok teşekkür ederim,*" I give you much thanks, I said, of course.

"*Bir şey değil, hanım efendi.*" It is nothing, ma'am, he said. The traffic waited.

"*Allahaismarladik,*" the Turkish good-bye that means, "We are putting ourselves in the hands of God," I said, meaning it in the Istanbul traffic.

"*Güle, güle,*" he said, go happily.

At last the traffic moved again.

At times like these, and there are so many, Istanbul turns in pace to a country town. There are long walks there, and afternoons, like towns in the country in summer. It is a city of nearly ten million people that spreads from Europe to Asia, up the Bosporus, along the Sea of Marmara, up the Golden Horn.

I had thought of going to Turkey on my own, as I had done so long ago, with what I look back on now, knowing what I do, as somewhat comic courage. I had forgotten Turkish manners. I was met at the airport by the colleague of a friend of a friend. Already I was being handed from *arkadaş* to *arkadaş*—that word for friendship, one of the most important words in the Turkish language. It is a way of living, a self-expectation as old as the nomads, although the people who are so hospitable must have long forgotten why they do it. They just do it. It is as natural as kindness or anger. My new, solicitous friend,

Ziya, whose name means "luminous," was an elegant, young, English-speaking Istanbul University graduate.

He may never have read Ibn Battuta, the four-teenth-century traveler who was handed from *akhis* to *akhis,* an old Turkish world for the generous organizations of young men who followed the standards of *futawwa*—an ideal of nobility, honesty, loyalty, and courage—but he was following, without considering anything else, the same rules of hospitality.

Ibn Battuta wrote, "We found ourselves in a fine building, carpeted with beautiful Turkish carpets and lit by a large number of chandeliers of Iraqi glass. A number of young men stood in rows in the hall, wearing long shirts and boots, and each had a knife about two cubits long attached to a girdle around his waist. On their heads were white woolen bonnets, and attached to the peak of those bonnets was a piece of stuff a cubit long and two fingers in breadth. When they took their seats, every man removed his bonnet and set it down in front of him, and kept on his head another ornamental bonnet of silk or another material. When we took our places, they served up a great banquet followed by fruits and sweetmeats, after which they began to sing and dance. We were filled with admiration and were greatly astonished by their open-handedness and generosity."

Now the word is *arkadaş,* not *akhis,* but it has the same sense to it, and although my young friend was dressed in a beautifully tailored Western suit, the same sense of care was there, the same warm concern.

I had come, as we all do when we go to cities we have heard about so much, to find an Istanbul I already thought I knew—my city of presuppositions—whispers and memories of pashas and harems and sultans and girls with almond eyes, the Orient Express of Agatha Christie, the spies of Eric Ambler, the civilized letters of Lady Mary Wortley Montagu.

My favorite travel book is *Eothen,* by Alexander Kinglake, published in 1844. I expected the "Asiatic contentment" he found there, and the naive world of his pasha, whose ecstatic vision of European locomotives he had never seen was, ". . . their horses are flaming coals!—whirr! whirr! All by wheels! Whiz! whizz! all by steam!"

I found almost at once that I had been as naive as the pasha. I had forgotten, except intellectually, that shadowed behind it all, like a huge broken monument of memory, was Constantinople, the Byzantine Empire of Constantine the Great, Justinian and Theodora, Julian the Apostate. In the fifteenth century, Mehmet the Conqueror captured it, and moved the capital of the young Ottoman Empire from Bursa and called the ancient city Istanbul.

It has one of the most familiar skylines in the world, but it is still a mystery. That is partly because of age, and partly because it is a monument to four men who changed the faces of the cities and of borders, and the way the eye sees, yet who have been almost forgotten.

There they are, standing out against the sky over Istanbul. The first, nearest the confluence of the Golden Horn, the Sea of Marmara, and the Bosporus, thrusts up against the sky, one of the oldest and most magic of buildings. Hagia Sophia, built by the Emperor Justinian, who, in his long reign—from A.D. 527 to 565—built buildings that stretched all over the Byzantine Empire, and changed it forever. The second, the Mosque of Süleyman, honors two men: Süleyman the Magnificent, and Sinan, the architectural genius who captured light and changed the way both the Middle East and Europe looked at buildings. The third is the mosque that is the monument to Mehmet the Conqueror, who rode into a nearly ruined and long neglected Constantinople, repaired it, rebuilt it, and changed its name to Istanbul.

We drove past the great walls of Theodosius, then along the walls that are all that is left, except for fragments, of the first palace of the Byzantine emperors. We turned through one of the ancient gates and up the narrow road toward the Sublime Porte. We entered a maze of uphill streets, a welter of turns and horns and tombs and mosques and markets and people.

Istanbul is not the only place to have great monuments and the memory of great men, a city pulse like no other, its own sense of excitement. It has all of these but, beyond them, it has wonderful neighborhoods and streets, streets full of people, streets used as markets, with snarls of traffic beyond anything I have seen in any other city, with drivers who are incredibly polite and pedestrians who obey no laws, not even those of survival. I saw a taxi driver patiently instructing two lost country people who were walking down the middle of the street while we waited in heavy traffic and a snarl of drivers honked like furious geese.

Ziya took me to a line of pastel-painted Ottoman houses on the cobblestone Street of the Cold Fountain. The old houses there have all been restored and combined into an inn called, appropriately, Aya Sofya Pansiyonlari, since it looks out on the building built by Justinian in the sixth century as the Church of the Hagia Sophia, the Holy Wisdom, and changed by Mehmet the Conqueror in 1532 into the mosque now called Aya Sofya. The houses use the great wall of Mehmet's palace of Topkapi ai their back walls.

As soon as I got to my room I called home, to Virginia. Somehow it seemed, not new, but old and right, to call the person I love most from Byzantium.

If there is a heart of the city, I found it in that little walking street between its two greatest monuments. Between the Byzantine Empire and the Ottoman, in front of my Ottoman house, I strolled at the pace of the Turks, which all the tourists seem to catch. To hurry and scrabble seemed silly and rude.

At dawn, the first call to prayer came from the Blue Mosque, and was echoed, fainter and fainter in the distance, from minarets all over the city of mosques. The gulls rose up in clouds from their perches on the roofs of Hagia Sophia and flew toward the water just beyond Topkapi, where the Sea of Marmara meets the Bosporus and the Golden Horn. They came back to roost there and flew among the minarets; their wings turned pink in the spotlights that illuminate the mosque at night.

Hagia Sophia seems to float there, on the hill that was the ancient acropolis of Byzantium, above the meeting of three waters: the Bosporus, the Sea of Marmara, the Golden Horn.

It has been the font of three empires. Here emperors and sultans were crowned, first the Byzantine Romans, and then the terrible Latins who decimated it in the Fourth Crusade and formed the short-lived Latin Empire. Here Mehmet II, child of the Osmanli Turks, ordered the blood of the slain washed from the marble floor, and had his name read as sultan at the first prayer in the new mosque of Aya Sofya.

Aya Sofya is a museum now, a new monument to the secular leader Atatürk, whose personal hatred of the clergy has left a void in Turkey that threatens to be filled dangerously.

More than a museum, too—I have walked many times through its great doors, and I have never heard a voice raised. The first sight of its captured space of golden light and twilight is more than breathtaking. I can only use the overused word: awe, an experience of awe.

The building covers more than four acres. It is wider than a football field is long, and yet there is not the overpowering sense of diminishment and human frailty that I find in the great dark spaces of the Gothic cathedrals. It is like walking into a field that contains the last sunset, under a dome that is a reflection of the sky, in the golden light of an early evening after a sunny day; a dome that rises to the height of a fifteen-story building and yet seems to shelter and not to intimidate. Most of the gold is gone, and the earliest mosaics were destroyed by the Iconoclasts between A.D. 729 and 843. The wall mosaics you see today were inlaid in the tenth century, some so high they seem to fly above you, some as intimate as portraits at the level of your eyes. The Holy Virgin looks down from the crown of the apse, so gentle on her golden chair that she seems just to have paused there for a little while to rest. Over the middle door of the inner narthex, called the imperial door and larger than the others, a tenth-century Christ receives obeisance from the kneeling emperor, supposedly Leo the Wise, who, according to the street joke of the time, was asking forgiveness for his many marriages.

Inlaid designs of marble veneer still make the walls into a patterned play of color from all over what was then the Roman Empire.

Dark green marble columns hold up the balconies so that they seem to soar. Some of these tall columns are said to have come from the temple of Artemis at Ephesus, and if so they would link the Hagia Sophia to the temple of the Asian Mother Goddess, all the way back to the Amazons.

But the controversy among scholars is almost as old as the story. Justinian did send out orders that marble should be brought from all over the empire for his church, and much was brought from the earthquake-broken city of Ephesus. The best explanation of how the legend rose is found in Selwyn Lloyd's *Ancient Turkey*. He says that the Artemision, one of the Seven Wonders of the ancient world, had already long been so lost to earthquake and silt and the reuse of marble by the sixth century, that it was thought that the gymnasium, the only large building left partly standing, was the temple. The columns may well have come from there.

Maybe so, but sometimes legends are truer than facts. From a prehistoric grove on the Aegean, where the Amazons clashed their shields and sang as the women do in *The Bacchae*, to the great temple of Artemis that grew there, to the Church of Hagia Sophia, the mosque of Aya Sofya, the museum, and to the first morning I saw it, is only a step, a dream of a night in archetypal terms. To legend and to me, they are the columns that once were in the place sacred to the great Anatolian Mother Goddess, so old that for centuries she needed no name.

The walls of the church were once covered with mosaic portraits of Byzantine rulers, but few of them are left. One is the Empress Zoë who, having been a virgin until she inherited the purple in her fifties, took to marriage as if she had invented it, and when she changed consorts, only the head on the mosaic of her coruler was changed, so that her last husband looks a little like one of those pictures you can have taken at the fair, when you stick your head through a hole and become Garbo or Scarlett O'Hara or the latest pop star.

Vague bishops look down from high above the second row of columns, and on all four squinches that help hold up the great dome there are huge cherubim with their folded blue wings. They have never been covered over, not by the Iconoclasts, who in their puritan zeal destroyed so much of Byzantine imagery, nor the Muslims, who do not allow any replica of the human figure. They have been restored through the centuries. Perhaps they were too high for the early reformers to reach, and when the church was made into a mosque, the Muslims still believed in fields of angels.

Although thousands of people troop though the building day after day, believers and unbelievers, there is a quiet corner of Hagia Sophia left, a niche out of time. Up on the north balcony, gentle in the sun of one of the windows, there are fragments, faces, a part of a robe, a hand intact and lifted in blessing—a sacred icon of a tragic Christ with a mourning Virgin on one side and John the Baptist on the other.

Across from it on the floor is the tomb of the Venetian Doge, Enrico Dandolo, who, nearly ninety and blind, was the first Venetian ashore at the capture and sack of Constantinople by the Crusaders in 1204. When the Byzantines returned, after nearly sixty years, it is said they took the bones of Dandolo and threw them to the dogs in the street.

Once the colors were dazzling. Now in that vast and grand simplicity, there is the subtlety of age, a visual echo. Thousands of people from all over the world visit Aya Sofya every day, as they have done since it was built. But now, instead of the voices of Goths and Latins, and rough Galatians, and traders from Cathay, instead of the shaggy skin trousers of the Scythians, the togas of the Romans from the west, the white robes of the Arab tribes, the stiff gold-laden caftans of the Byzantines, the silk shifts of the traders from China, there are English voices, and German, and French, and Japanese, tourists dressed in clothes that seem in modern times to be all alike, a world of jeans and T-shirts, and the man-made textiles of traveling clothes in chemical colors. There is a sprinkling of women in black *yaşmaks* from the Arab countries, where ever since it was the Caliphate and the Ottoman Sultan was also the Caliph of Islam, Istanbul has been one of the centers of the Muslim world.

But there is a more surprising monument to Justinian, and it would certainly seem so to him. In 532 he ordered that columns that were still lying, unused, from the broken, abandoned pagan temples that had fallen to neglect and riot and earthquake, and the change of religion, be used to hold up the roof of an underground cistern. The columns were the flotsam of the past that littered Constantinople. It was an engineering job, part of the water system, no more. For years, since long before the Ottoman takeover of the city, the cistern was forgotten, which probably saved it from being used yet again as material for rebuilding.

There are 336 of these columns. The thousands of tons of silt that had nearly buried them have been cleared out; the long rows that are as near to being like a Roman temple as can be found anywhere are uncovered in the half darkness, and their presentation is one of the theatrical triumphs of the showing of ancient monuments. Theatrical—yes—but the light and sound captures its magic. Lights flirt and change from the distance, open vistas darken them again. It is totally romantic. I seem to be, and I knew I was not, discovering it for myself.

The columns seem to go into an infinity of darkness. I passed one that was the twin of one I had seen up in the street where once the Forum of Augustus stood. They had been carved like tree trunks with the branches lopped; the lopped places looked like eyes. One upside down, one on her side, two sad Medusas, that had once guarded temples from the evil eye, had been underwater for centuries. They are now partially out of the water, and they are tinged with color from the long drowning. They lie there, looking out into the dark. The music is Beethoven, and it should be: Only that heroic sound could match the gaunt majesty of the marble forest that the Turks call the Underground Palace.

Within the crowded quietness of the first hill— the overwhelming mixture of Greek, Roman, Byzantine, Ottoman empires—the Sultan Ahmet Camii, called the Blue Mosque by Westerners, is directly across the park flanked by a classic courtyard. Over the hill to the left, to be hunted in the poor streets with their tumbling wooden houses is all that remains, according to ancient travelers, of the greatest imperial palace ever built on earth. It was so looted by the Christian Europeans of the Fourth Crusade that, three hundred years later, when Mehmet rode through it on his entry into Constantinople, it was already an abandoned ruin. I walked along nearly deserted streets in the sunny morning, and children with voices like doves, who know two words, "hello" and "good-bye," said them both, usually at the same time.

On the other side of the Blue Mosque there is a long park with three columns in a line down the middle. On one of them a stone emperor with a stone court watches a chariot race long gone. It is the old Hippodrome, where the great rivalries of the Blues and the Greens turned from the backing of chariot teams into politics and martyrdom, and where the Empress Theodora worked as a circus girl and whore.

This place is soaked with sanctity and blood. To go down below the end of the park is to pass by what is left of the huge Hippodrome wall, pierced with houses, and with gates that no longer go any place, with caves that once were rooms. I walked, or climbed, up the ruined wasteland of a hill, among the fragments and the gravelike mounds, and looked for ghosts of the palace of the Caesars.

It was an eerie search. Where once there were courtiers, a vagrant stared out from his shelter, an arch, nearly filled with earth, that had once been a high regal arch of the palace. Time had made it a cave for squatters. He watched from the darkness of the cave like a wild animal. It was the only time in Istanbul, in all the days and nights of walking, that I was afraid.

Some idea of what it may have been like, in color and in wit, can be found in the little Mosaic Museum, a work of the Australian archaeologists and the Australian government, who realize that these are monuments that belong to the world, and as such deserve what help foundations and scholarship can give the Turkish government to look after this rich heritage. Turkey has been looted so often through the centuries, that it is more than a disgrace if our own organizations, supposedly dedicated to their study, join in the theft and the neglect.

There are two contrasts—Hagia Sophia, one of the greatest of Byzantine Christian monuments, has so little money that sometimes the work of renovation and maintenance has to stop for months. No foundation has offered help with it. On the other hand, at the Church of Saint Saviour in Chora at the other end of the old city near the walls of Theodosius, the mosaics have been superbly restored by the American Institute of Byzantine Research and the Turkish Touring and Automobile Club, which is responsible for saving much of Ottoman Istanbul as well.

To walk into it is to walk into the color and zest of the late flowering of Byzantine art, when the Iconoclasts had at last been defeated and the formal mosaics of the early Byzantines had been forgotten for two hundred years. The figures seem to move, have depth, glow. The walls are a study of the time just before the final fall of the empire, a last spark of full life. They are contemporary with Giotto, and one wonders what the Renaissance, which had been partly fomented by discoveries in Anatolia, would have brought to Constantinople had it not fallen.

But it was only when I went to Italy a few months after being in Istanbul that I found sixth-century Byzantium, untouched by the Iconoclasts, and the loot from Constantinople taken away by the soldiers of Enrico Dandolo. Ravenna has today the only sixth-century Byzantine mosaics left in the world. It had been an outpost of the Byzantine Empire, and when the Iconoclast soldiers came on orders from the eighth-century puritan Emperor Leo, to destroy the church art, the city revolted. I had the rare experience of seeing the city for the first time so soon after being at the source of the Byzantine Empire, so much of which they inadvertently saved, that I felt that I had come from Byzantium instead of modern Istanbul.

High in the center of the apse of San Vitale in Ravenna, a young, unbearded Christ sits on a round blue sphere that floats in a gold sky, and the rivers of life flow from the green mosaic land below him. On either side of the apse are two of the most famous mosaic imperial portraits in the world.

There, beyond all that has been written of them, beyond the scurrilous gossip and the adulation, I found Justinian and Theodora, the emperor and the Evita Perón of her time, staid as only an actress imitating an empress could be.

Justinian's hair is red, his slight pudginess is there, a double chin, a pursed mouth, ruddy cheeks, under the heavy jewels of the imperial insignia. He looks oddly tentative. Trained to be emperor better than most of the Byzantines, the man who never slept, who lived like an anchorite, who rebuilt the city of Constantinople, who was the most perfect civil servant who ever graced the Byzantine throne, Justinian watches Theodora as he must have done in life, looking for some sign of approval in her imperious, sad face. He was in his mid-sixties when San Vitale was built, but not in this mosaic portrait.

In her portrait, Theodora is regal, beautiful, watchful. She would die three months after the mosaic was placed there. She was a woman of pride far beyond sheer vanity, and she would not have sent a portrait of herself aging and dying. Since there is so much guessing by scholars about the dates of the mosaics, I will guess too, but I will guess from human instinct and not from the age of stones. I think that she approved these portraits, and that she sent the best Byzantine royal artists to install them and surround them with the gold-backed colored glass and perhaps gems that make them up. She knew how to be an empress.

But in the church of Saint Apollinaire Nuovo, where long lines of virgins and martyrs march in procession toward Christ on one side and the Holy Mother on the other, and where the three wise men almost dance toward the Christ Child, there is another portrait of Justinian that has confounded scholars, too, since it was discovered a century ago. The church was decorated with those elegant formal mosaics only a few years after San Vitale, but Theodora was dead, and this Justinian has grown fat, his hair is white, yet the tentative look is still there. She was adored as few women have ever been worshipped, and he is alone and doesn't care whether he is old or young or that his hair is white. He is only waiting out the rest of his long, lonely reign.

When I went to the eleventh-century San Marco in Venice I found even more of the glory and color of Constantinople in hints and imitation and loot. The wild-frontier Venetians copied San Marco from the Church of the Apostles, built by Justinian in what had been their mother city, Constantinople, and to which they still looked for art, for riches. They constructed, as provincial people do, as we build Gothic spires of Georgian chapels, an instant past by copying a church already four hundred years old.

In 1204 the Venetians nearly destroyed the great Constantinople that they had envied for so long. For centuries the bronze and gold horses that they stole from the Hippodrome stood over the center doors of San Marco. They have meant Venice to the world, caught there in the sun in silent neigh and pace. Now the horses outside the church are replicas. The originals have been moved inside the museum to protect them from the modern corrosive air.

All around me there were Byzantine gold sacred objects, silks, vestments. The treasure room was full of gold objects from Hagia Sophia that had escaped being melted down by Napoleon. The icon of the Madonna Nicopeia, the Bearer of Victory, that was carried before the Byzantine army, and that had so failed them when the Fourth Crusade took the city, stood in a chapel by the high altar. The Byzantine crucifix with its twisted body of an agonized Christ that they say bled when one of the crusading marauders stabbed it with his sword, was two feet from me at mass, and I could have touched it.

The mosaic floor that heaves like frozen waves; the incense from the East; the darkened shadows in the corners of the church's cruciform shape, covered to its domes with late Byzantine mosaics; all the gold-backed and jewel-colored glass catching the candlelight; the great alter where they say the body of Saint Mark himself, stolen from Alexandria, still rests; and even the altar floor, said to be the rock where the Christ stood to preach the Beatitudes; all these treasures surrounded me in this pirates' church, glittering with ancient loot.

The shapes are in Istanbul, the great stone edifices, but the color, the jewels, the curious intimacy, the personalities of Justinian and Theodora, the glorious fragments from grand imperial worship, are there in Italy, a hint and a memory of the city that was called, in the sixth century, the richest city in Christendom.

On the first evening that I was in Istanbul I walked out into the park between the Aya Sofya and the Blue Mosque, which stands on the ground where the

Imperial Palace once stood. I found a man with two fawns, as delicate as Persian paintings. He was letting them crop the grass. The people from the crowded, poor neighborhoods of wooden houses, tilted with age over the hill amid the ruins of the Imperial Palace of the Caesars, had flocked, whole families, to the spacious walks and gardens. By evening, the tourists were mostly gone. Istanbul had become Turkish again.

The Turks were using the city as they would have used the villages that man of them came from: as outdoor living rooms where they visited, strolled, or sat and watched the *son et lumière* at the Blue Mosque and listened to Turkish poetry being read in tragic lilting voices into a microphone, not because they especially cared about poetry, but because it was there and they are a polite people and it was evening and the poets were trying and it is a tradition all the way back to Nasrettin Hoca to listen to storytellers, declaiming their stories in the *miş* tense, *bir var miş, bir yok miş,* maybe it happened, maybe it didn't.

On the following morning, after the quiet people and the poetry I could not understand—only the lilt and passion of it—after the most awe-inspiring building I had ever seen, I sat with a heavy-minded civil servant who had offered me tea because I was a foreign writer. He sat there explaining the obvious, when an old man, threadbare, proud, came by selling his poetry. It was printed on thin pink paper, and it had in it the images of the old Ottoman court or Divan poetry, grown as thin as the paper, half starved and discounted. He must have been eighty years old, the poet, and it was a love poem, about the almond eyes of *houris,* and about long black hair, and windows and veils of morning and hidden faces. I bought the thin little broadsheet, and we smiled at each other like friends. He reminded me of the people that I had found in the work of Sait Faik, whose stories about the streets and the people of Istanbul are the finest prose I know in modern Turkey. He is Turkey's Chekhov. Alas, too few have been translated, and so Sait Faik must wait for a translator to release his Istanbul for Western readers.

The old poet would have talked with me but when he saw a man who so obviously represented government, he looked down and thanked me politely and went away. Turks don't like government, whatever it is. They have, at least the poor, a residue of ancient fear. When I gave him the equivalent of fifty cents, the civil servant said it was too much, that he was a beggar who had too much pride to beg, so he sold the broadsheets. I said, "*Yok,*" the magnificent final negative of the Turks, "he is a poet." I did not tell him that I had more in common with the threadbare writer than I did with him, but I too had caught, from my hungry friend, a little of his fear.

But he, and the Ottoman love poem, had drawn me out of the deep past, and made me ready to walk into the Istanbul of Mehmet the Conqueror. Cities have levels of time, and I find myself, like a mushroom hunter in a field who doesn't see anything after a while but mushrooms, able to concentrate my vision on a period of time, and keep it there until I walk out again into the present. At least I thought it was so until I walked in Istanbul, and kept stumbling over a present as pulsing with life as any past there has ever been.

I went to nearby Topkapı, a vast intimacy of stone tents with walls of bright tile and veins of gold— pavilions and gardens, retreats and follies and space. Its jeweled pavilions are sparsely furnished, as if the Ottoman sultans remembered in their souls that they had been nomads and must be ready to move along. I saw this over and over later in Ottoman houses: not poverty—far from that—but cupboards that could be emptied quickly, beds that could be rolled away. An echo of tent living in wonderful, wood-carved rooms.

Oh, all that I expected of Ottoman excess was there at Topkapı, and more—the jewels as big as hens' eggs, the aigrettes made of feathers and diamonds, the fine chinaware that had been encrusted with precious stones as if it had caught a disease of riches, the jeweled hasps of daggers, the gold boxes, the walls of tile and gold in the cozy, one-roomed pavilions.

The Ottoman reputation for intrigue and for murder is there, too, in the Harem, a clutched warren of rooms, baths, and courtyards. But no romantic horror story can convey the claustrophobia and the beauty of the place. It is a huge, ornate prison for women, and for many of the sultans, who hid there in fear of their lives, victims of the irony of absolute rule. There is, in all that rich imperial polyglot, no place to be alone.

I set out to find a clue to what life in the Harem must have been like, for nothing is dead in Istanbul. Yesterday and today are intertwined every place. There are two seventeenth-century Turkish baths, *hamams,* where guidebooks written by men promise marble floors and steam-misted tiled rooms with ancient columns. In both of the historic *hamams,* I had only a glimpse of the imposing entrance to the main baths, all for men. The women's section is entered through a very unassuming side door.

I expected to be brought Turkish coffee, and to be wrapped in thick, warm Turkish towels. Instead I was shoved into a cold, dirty cubicle, given a thin towel, and told to undress. The attendant pointed to a door with her cigarette.

Inside, the room was domed and vaguely warm. In the center there was a raised platform. Around the sides were basins with very hot running water, but instead of the brass bowls I had expected, there were plastic dog bowls.

At one of the basins an enormously fat naked old woman, with arms of iron, was sitting washing her underwear. She was the attendant, a eunuch figure, pendulous and mighty. They are an ancient guild, those masseuses, and for the first time I had a sense that I was in a room that might have been like the reality instead of the romance of the Harem.

She lumbered over to me, forced me down onto the low ledge and, without a word, began to scrub me with a loofah, harder than I have ever been scrubbed in my life. Dirt came off in rolls of black. She then washed my hair and poured basin after basin of very hot water over me, hair, head, body, and all. I could not be anything but passive. It was like being bathed as a small child by an angry mother. She grabbed an arm and held it high while she soaped my armpit. She grabbed a leg and scrubbed it as if she were taking barnacles off a keel.

Then she motioned me to the raised platform of stone, and proceeded to beat me up. It wasn't fat on her arms, it was muscles. Finally I was able to escape. She waddled after me with a towel around her middle, looking like a wrestler on television, and demanded *bahşiş*, a tip, the only time I ever heard the word in the nine weeks I was in Turkey.

I got out of the place as fast as I could. I walked down the steep ancient street called Fish Street, where the music shops are clustered in the Turkish way of having all the same kinds of shops together, and then to the Galata Tower. I suddenly realized that I was more relaxed than I could ever remember. Across the Galata Bridge and then along the Roman walls at the Sea of Marmara, I wandered in a stream of people.

When I want comfort, cosseting, I will not go to a *hamam,* but I still suspect that I was nearer to the atmosphere and the treatment in the Harem than I will ever be again. There may be singing and dancing and gossip in the *hamam*—the guidebooks say so—but not in that place and not that day, even though I was told it was the most famous *hamam* in Istanbul, and that Florence Nightingale had been beaten up there, too.

The Ottomans did not destroy Constantinople; they rebuilt it as Istanbul. Mehmet II repaired its bridges, its water supplies, turned its churches into mosques, and what we see today of the Byzantine culture is there because of the protection of the Ottomans who came later.

I was guided through much of this by one of the finest guidebooks I have ever seen of any city except Kyoto. It is called *Strolling Through Istanbul,* written by two teachers at the local Robert College, Hilary Sumner-Boyd and John Freely. They share in it their years of discovering Istanbul. I used it in my own way, taking the book, following it for a while, getting lost in the labyrinthine streets, and discovering for myself, as they had done. I still read it, knowing where it leads, and I am back in Istanbul, wandering through that intimate, imperial, small, huge city.

Then, as they had done, over and over, I stumbled on treasures, tumbles of old buildings, antheaps of people working as they always had, here in an abandoned basilica, there in a *han,* a pious foundation for travelers founded by the Valide Sultan, the mother of one of the sultans in the seventeenth century, now full of the noise and smell of printing and tanning. Shiite Muslims from Iran, who have been there for centuries, looked up with blackened faces from their work, stripped to the waist in the heat, and greeted me as politely as if it were still a *han,* instead of a conglomerate of factories and shops.

On the low wall, which is all that is left of one of the Byzantine mansions, a young man sat beside a professional letter writer, who had placed his typewriter where the round atrium had once been. He was pouring out his inarticulate heart, so that the letter writer would translate it into the suitable, flowery prose of an ardent love letter.

Sometimes, early in the morning when the streets were still almost deserted, I would say good morning to the shopkeepers setting up their shops, the peddlers with their wonderfully colored vegetable and fruit carts, the children with their hello–good-byes. Some of them, a little bolder, would ask if I was German or French or English, and when I got tired of that, I told them I had come from the moon the night before—but I told them in the *mış* tense for fairy tales and possibilities.

In all the early morning walks I saw only one person who had slept out of doors. No matter how poor Turkish people are, they look after their own. To do anything else would bring shame to their extended families. He was a young man with a fine, new Harley-Davidson motorcycle. He slept on a bench near the wall below the Palace of the Caesars. His motorcycle was chained to his leg.

Later, I struggled through the crowds along Divan Yolu in Sultanahmet, which leads to Beyazit Square, where the fifteenth-century mosque of Sultan Beyazit II towers over the Grand Bazaar, started in the sixteenth, now grown over acre after acre of Beyazit, until today you must push through an international crowd of drifters and shoppers under several miles of domed and vaulted ceilings.

There it is, the essence of mercantile Istanbul, more than four thousand shops and thousands of merchants. I think of it as the lungs and not the heart of the city. It is, and always has been, a huge commercial mart since it was started as a warehouse, probably for the old palace, built there by Mehmet when he found the imperial palace of the Caesars in ruins. He soon left it to the merchants and the retainers, and built Topkapi, on the hill overlooking the three waters that come together below it.

Under the high vaulted ceilings, in a maze of turns and secret places, there is covered street after covered street of glory and kitsch, gold and brass, transistors and hookahs, copper and plastic, silk and shoddy, and outside, in one of the astonishing quiet corners between the bazaar and the mosque, I found a print of a painting of Süleyman the Law Giver, careening his horse under the arches of one of the same cobbled streets I had just come from. Among the crowd of students in blue jeans and T-shirts from the university that stands where Mehmet's first palace stood, a beggar from the *Arabian Nights* huddled at one of the many bazaar doors, saying, "Alms for the love of Allah."

Here, as in every place I went in Turkey, I walked into the past, and into a kind of peace that must have been there for so long when there was a sense of sacredness around the mosques. Beyond the wall that shuts a courtyard of the mosque from the street, there was not a voice raised, not a single frantic, "Please madam, buy leather!" Away from the noise and frantic buying and selling, grabbing and coaxing, of the street, there are tables set up under old trees, and when I walked through the gate I walked into an oasis of calm.

There old men were selling rings and knives and jewelry from what I suspect was their own family's poor inheritance, goods that we call ethnic for lack of a more complimentary term. It was a pool of honesty and quiet bargaining.

Small boys brought chained brass trays of tea to the sellers, and old men left over from revolution and Ottoman manners walked hand in hand with friends they had had since childhood, meticulous men, with their cracked shoes kept polished and their clean shirts, living too long on too little, walking together under the trees. There is a lot of physical contact between men in Turkey. They hold hands. They kiss. They walk with their arms entwined. It is somehow more masculine, more quietly dignified, than our habits of physical avoidance, as if we were afraid to touch.

This is a part of the sense of intimacy I miss and always will; they made me part of it. Even after nine weeks back in Turkey, when I returned to Washington and a clerk was rude to me in a hotel, I had become so used to that easy politeness that I started to cry from shock.

Beyond the mosque, there is a seventeenth-century abandoned *hamam,* where the old had made what was once the new, and remnants of a frieze of Roman soldiers are a part of the wall, some of them upside down.

But when I turned away from the crowds in the main streets, there were the secret spaces: chickens wandering the grounds of mosques, vegetable gardens, flowers and dogs, and always the children who said hello–goodbye. I stopped for a smiling crowd of children in a crocodile, going to school. There are still, as there always have been, hundreds of neighborhoods that are like villages, with the same politeness, the same quietness, that I found farther east in Anatolia.

Because of these areas of simplicity, Istanbul has another quality that very few large cities have. It has afternoons, long lazy ones like when I was a child. On an afternoon like that I walked with a friend along the wall of Theodosius at the extreme eastern end of the old city.

The only reminder of frantic Istanbul was the line of fast cars coming through Edirne Kapi, the Adrianople Gate that Mehmet the Conqueror rode through on 29 May 1453, in royal turban and sky-blue boots, some say with a rose in his hand, some say the sword of Mohammed, at the head of a Muslim army shouting, "Halt not conquerors! God be praised! We are the conquerors of Constantinople!"

A beautiful chestnut horse was tethered in a small open meadow below the wall, its owner unaware that it grazed where the Emperor's horses were once kept. Children played on the swings of a playground over a part of what is left of the last palace of the Caesars, and their mothers gossiped and smiled where once Byzantine women did, looking out over the Golden Horn.

There was a small part of the last palace complex of the Caesars, the Blachernae; its snaggled towers and some of its walls with windows that are open gaps are all that still stand, but beside them, surviving, is a pure reminder of Byzantium, a small palace, its Byzantine brick outer walls with their bicolored designs almost intact. It is without a floor, but its walls, its arches, and its courtyard have survived. It is Tekfur Serayı, the Palace of the Sovereign. It has been a warehouse, a factory, a zoo, and now it stands, an empty shell.

It is kept by a woman who also keeps goats, and who welcomed us as if the palace, not the small hut she lived in, were her home. At the top of the wall that made a closed meadow for her in front of the last fine facade, we could see all the way to the Sea of Marmara, along that great skyline of Mehmet and Süleyman and Sinan and Justinian.

Ottoman Istanbul is honored and reflected by that one great soldier turned architect, Sinan, who lived from 1491 to 1588. He was a member of the Janissary Corps, the elite body of soldiers taken from Christian families as small children and raised in the imperial court as Muslims and guards of the sovereign, who became in time the most feared soldiers in the empire. The Muslim children, captured or bought in the same way by the Crusaders and raised as Christians, were known as the Turkopolier. Sinan was a military engineer until his fifties with Süleyman tapped him to be his official architect, an act of patronage like the Pope demanding Michelangelo's presence in Rome.

Any city that has such an architect has its own immortality. There are forty-one of his buildings still standing. The Haseki Hürrem Hamami, built for Süleyman in honor of his wife, the Frenchwoman known in the west as Roxelana, is across the paved yard-cum-street in front of Hagia Sophia. It is now a museum and salesroom for Turkish carpets, and is beautifully restored in all its Ottoman whiteness.

Within the outer walls of Hagia Sophia is one of the saddest and most beautiful of Sinan's buildings. It is the tomb he built for Sultan Selim II in 1577. It is covered with delicate, multicolored İznik tiles, used as mosaic pieces to make large patterns of trees, plants, abstract designs. It is now being restored after the nineteenth-century thievery by an Istanbul dentist, who stole one of the superb wall plaques on its facade and sold it to the West. His fake replacement is already faded, but on the other side of the door, the original tiles of Sinan seem to have been put there yesterday.

The interior is full of that strange diffused glow from window-pierced walls that Sinan created in all his buildings, made not to see out of, but to let in light. There, in tiny catafalques the size of children's beds, are thirty-two children of Selim, murdered in the royal way inherited from the Seljuks, with the silken bowstring, to insure the succession of Murat, the eldest son. It was Ottoman custom, to keep civil war from breaking out at the death of a monarch, but afterward there was such grief that the silken bowstring was replaced in time by lifetime imprisonment among the women of the Harem, of princes who might revolt and claim the sultanate.

It was on that afternoon at the walls of Theodosius that I found what to me was the jewel of that genius of an architect, the Mosque of Mihrimah, the daughter of Süleyman, on the hill near Edirne Kapi.

Sinan and Mihrimah—I think of walls that are stone strong and let the light in like lace, of space within that has the same quality as that of Hagia Sophia, even more light because the interiors are so simple and the clear walls so pierced with windows and so high. He created gentle spaces, sheltering without diminishing, soaring without losing a sense of the human, and alive with color, always color, refined and glowing, and filled with quietness. Here, in the Mosque of Mihrimah, is the simplicity of Islam that in other hands can turn to boredom, but not with Sinan, not with his genius for capturing light and space and letting them both soar upward.

In the great Mosque of Süleyman, the men go on praying in the magnificent space, undaunted by the thousands of tourists, some of whom sit in a circle in the entry, being lectured in several languages by their guides about Sinan, whose name means spearhead, one of the great architects of the world, about whom they have probably never heard.

It is all Istanbul, as polite and friendly as a country village, as noisy and clotted with people as any city in the world, old, and sleepy, and busy. I felt, not welcomed, but taken for granted there. They are used to so many strangers. For more than fifteen hundred years of empire, Istanbul has welcomed an international horde from whatever the known world was and is.

Crowded, dirty Istanbul; blowsy, insouciant. I thought of Simone Signoret in *Ship of Fools*, more exciting, beautiful, fascinating than a younger woman without her wise seductiveness could ever be.

Ottaviano Bon

SULTAN AHMET I CHOOSES A BEDFELLOW

. . . IF HE SHOULD require one of them for his pleasure or to watch them at play or hear their music, he makes known his desire to the Head Kadin, who immediately sends for the girls who seem to her to be the most beautiful in every respect and arranges them in a line from one end of the room to the other. She then brings in the King, who passes before them once or twice, and according to his pleasure fixes his eyes on the one who attracts

---

Ottaviano Bon was the Venetian diplomat to the Ottoman sultan of Constantinople in 1605. This is excerpted from his rather lively diaries from this stay.

him the most, and as he leaves throws one of his handkerchiefs into her hand, expressing the desire to sleep the
night with her. She, having this good fortune, makes up
as well as she can and, coached and perfumed by the
Kadin, sleeps the night with the King in the Royal chamber in the women's apartments, which is always kept ready
for such an event. And while they are sleeping the night
the Kadin arranges for some old Moorish women, who
take it in turn to stay in the room for two or three hours
at a time. There are always two torches burning there, one
at the door of the room, where one of the old women is,
and the other at the foot of the bed; and they change
without making a sound, so that the King is not disturbed
in any way. On rising in the morning the King changes all
his clothes, leaving the girl those he was wearing with all
the money that was in the purses: then, going to his other
rooms, he sends her a present of clothes, jewels, and
money in accordance with the satisfaction and pleasure
received. The same procedure holds good for all the oth-

ers who take his fancy, lasting longer with one than with another according to the pleasure and affection he feels for her. And she who becomes pregnant is at once called Cassachi Sultan—that is to say, Queen Sultana—and if she bears a son its arrival is heralded with the greatest festivities.

Herman Melville

CONSTANTINOPLE JOURNAL

Thursday Dec 11th Thick fog during the night. Steamed very slowly, ringing the bell. Ere daylight came to anchor in the Sea of Marmora, as near as the Captain could determine, within but three miles or less of Constantinople. All day the fog held on. Very thick, & damp & raw. Very miserable for the Turks & their harrems; particularly when they were doused out by the deck-washing.

Herman Melville's sailing exploits provided the background for his many classics, including Moby Dick, Opoo, *and* Billy Budd. *The diaries from these adventures make for wild reading, too. This excerpt is from* A Visit to Europe and the Levant *(1857).*

Some sick & came below to the fire; off with their "ash-macks" & c. Several steamers at anchor around us, but invisable; heard the scream (alarms) of their pipes & ring-ing of bells. — During the second night, heard the Con-stantinople dogs barks & bells ring. Old Turk ("Old Sinope") I said to him "This is very bad" he answered "God's will is good," & smoked his pipe in cheerful resig-nation.

Friday Dec 12th. About noon fog slowly cleared away before a gentle breeze. At last, as it opened around us, we found ourselves lying, as in enchantment, among the Prince Islands, scores of vessels in our own predicament around us. [The] Invisable confounds. (Forgot to note that during the fog several "kyacks" came alongside, attracted by our bell. They had lost their way in the fog. They were Constantinople boats. One of them owned by a boy, who moored under our quarter & there went to sleep in the fog. Specimen of an oriental news boy. The self-possession & easy ways.) The first appearance of Constantinople from the sea is described as magnificent. See "Anastasius." But one lost this. The fog only lifted from about the skirts of the city, which being built upon a promontory, left the crown of it hidden wrapped in vapor. Could see the base & wall of St. Sophia but not the dome. It was a coy disclosure, a kind of coquetting, leaving room for imagination & heightening the scene. Constantinople, like her Sultanas, was thus seen veiled in her "ashmack." Magic effect of the lifting up of the fog disclosing such a city as Constantinople. — At last rounded Seraglio Point & came to anchor at 2 PM on the Golden Horn. Crossed over to Tophanna in a caique (like a canoe, but one end pointed out like a knife, covered with quaint carving, like old furniture). No demand made for passport nor any examination of luggage. Got a guide to Hotel du Globe in Pera. Wandered about a little before dinner. Dined at 6 P.M. 10 F[rancs] per day for 5th story room without a carpet & c. Staid in all night.

Dangerous going out, owing to footpads & assassins. The curse of these places. Can't go out at night, & no places to go to, if you could.

Saturday Dec 13th.   Up early; went out; saw cemeteries, where they dumped garbage. Sawing wood over a tomb. Forrests of cemeteries. Intricacy of the streets. Started alone for Constantinople and after a terrible long walk, found myself back where I started. Just like getting lost in a wood. No plan to streets. Pocket-compass. Perfect labyrinth. Narrow. Close, shut in. If one could but get *up* aloft, it would be easy to see one's way out. If you could get up into tree. Soar out of the maze. But no. No names to the streets no more than to natural allies among the groves. No numbers. No anything. — Breakfast at 10 A.M. Took guide ($1.25 per day) and started for a tour. Took caique for Seraglio. Holy ground. Crossed some extensive grounds & gardens. Fine buildings of the Saracenic style. Saw the Mosque of St.

Sophia. Went in. Rascally priests demanding "bakshesh."
Fleeced me out of 1/2 dollar; following me round, selling the fallen mosaics. Ascended a kind of horse way
leading up, round & round. Came out into a gallery fifty
feet above the floor. Supurb interior. Precious marbles
Porphyry & Verd antique. Immense magnitude of the
building. Names of the prophets in great letters. Roman
Catholic air to the whole. —— To the hippodrome, near
which stands the six towered mosque of Sultan Achmet;
soaring up with its snowy spires into the pure blue sky.
like light-houses. Nothing finer. In the Hippodrome saw
the obelisk with Roman inscription upon the base. Also
a broken monument of bronze, representing three twisted
serpents erect upon the tails. Heads broken off. Also a
square monument of masoned blocks. Leaning over &
frittered away — like an old chimny stack. A Greek
inscription shows it to [be] of the time of Theodosius.
Sculpture about the base of the obelisk, representing
Constantine, wife & sons, & c. Then saw the "Burnt

Column." Black & grimy enough & hooped about with iron. Stands soaring up from among a huddle of old wooden rookeries. A more striking fire monument than that of London. Then to the Cistern of 1001 columns. You see a rounded knoll covered with close herbage. Then a kind of broken cellar way, you go down, & find yourself on a wooden, rickety platform, looking down into a grove of marble pillars, fading away into utter darkness. A palatial sort of Tartarus. Two tiers of pillars one standing on t'other; lower tier half buried. Here & there a little light percolates through from breaks in the keys of the arches; where bits of green straggle down. Used to be a resivoir. Now full of boys twisting silk. Great hubbub. Flit about like imps. Whir of the spinning jennies. In going down, (as into a ship's hold) and wandering about, have to beware the innumerable skeins of silk. Terrible place to be robbed or murdered in. At whatever point you look, you see lines of pillars, like trees in an orchard arranged in the quincus style. —

Came out. Overhead looks like a mere shabby common, or worn out sheep pasture. — To the Bazarr. A wilderness of traffic. Furniture, arms, silks, confectionery, shoes, saddles — everything. Covered overhead with stone arches, with side openings. Immense crowds. Georgians, Armenians, Greeks, Jews & Turks are the merchants. Magnificent embroidered silks & gilt sabres & caparisons for horses. You loose yourself & are bewildered & confounded with the labyrinth, the din, the barbaric confusion of the whole. — Went to the Watch Tower within a kind of arsenal. (immense arsenal.) The Tower of vast girth & heigth in the Saracenic style — a column. From the top, my God, what a view! Surpasses everything. The Propontis, the Bosphorous, the Golden Horn, the domes the minarets, the bridges, the men of war, the cypresses. — Indescribable. — Went to the Pigeon Mosque. In its court the pigeons covered the pavement as thick as in the West they fly in hosts. A man feeding them. Some perched upon the roof of the collonades, & upon the fountain in the middle & on the cypresses. — Took off my shoes, & went in. Pigeons inside, flying round in the dome, in & out the lofty windows. — Went to Mosque of Sultan Sulyman. The third one in point of size & splendor. — The Mosque is a sort of marble marquee of which the minarets (four or six) are the stakes. In fact when inside it struck me that the idea of this kind of edifice was borrowed from the tent. Though it would make a noble ball room. — Off shoes & went in. This custom more sensible than taking off hat. Muddy shoes; but never muddly heads. Floor covered with mats & over them beautiful rugs of great size & square. Fine light coming through side slits below the dome. Blind dome. Many Turks at prayer; bowing heads to the floor towards a kind of alter. Chanting going on. In a gallery saw lot of portmanteaux chests & bags; as in a R.R. baggage car. Put there for safe-keeping by men who leave home, or afraid of robbers & taxation. "Lay not up your treasures where moth

& rust do corrupt." & c. Fountains (a row of them) outside along the sides of the mosque for bathing the feet
& hands of worshippers before going in. Natural rock.
— Instead of going in in stockings (as I did) the Turks
wear over shoes & doff them outside the mosque. —
The tent like form of the mosque broken up & diversi-
fied with infinite number of arches, buttresses, *small
domes, collonades* cupolas, &c &c &c. — Went down to
Golden Horn. Crossed bridge of pontoons. Stood in the
middle & not a cloud in the sky. Deep blue & clear.
Delightful elastic atmosphere, altho December. A kind of
English June cooled & tempered sherbet-like with an
American October; the serenity & beauty of summer
without the heat. — Came home through the vast suburbs of Galata & c. Great crowds of all nations —
money changers — *coins of all nations circulate* — Placards
in four or five languages; Turkish, French, Greek,
Armenian Lottery. advertisements of boats the same. *You
feel you are among the nations.* Great curse that of Babel; not

being able to talk to a fellow being, &c. — Have to
beware of your pockets. My guide went with his hands
to his. — The horrible grimy tragic air of these streets.
The rotten & wicked looking houses. So gloomy &
grimy seems as if a suicide hung from every rafter
within. — No open space — no squares or parks. You
suffocate for room. — You pass close together. The
cafes of the Turks. Dingey holes, faded splendor, moth
eaten, on both sides wide seats or divans where the old
musty Turks sit smoking like conjurers. — Saw in certain kiosks (pavilions) the crowns of the late Sultans.
You look through gilt gratings & between many curtains
of lace, at the sparkling things. Near the mosque of Sultan Solyman saw the cemetery of his family — big as
that of a small village, all his wives & children & servants. All gilt & carved. The women's tombs carved
without heads (women no souls). The Sultan Solyman's
tomb & that of his three brothers in a kiosk. Gilded like
mantle ornaments.

Sunday Dec. 14. Three Sabbaths a week in Constantino-ple. Friday, Turks; Sat, Jews; Sunday, Romanists, Greeks, & Armenians. — At 8 AM crossed over the 2d bridge to Stamboul to ride round the Walls. Passed between wall & Golden Horn through Greek & Jew quarters, and came outside the land wall in view of Sweet Waters, which run inland & end in beautiful glades. Rode along the land wall. By this wall Constantinople was taken by the Turks & the last of the Constantines fell in their defence. Four miles of massiveness, with huge square towers — a Tower of London — every 150 yards or so. In many parts rent by earthquakes. The towers especially. Great cracks & fis-sures. In one tower you see a jaw of light opening; the riven parts stand toppling like inverted pyramids. Ever-green vines mantling them. 4 walls parallel — added defences. The strength of the masonry shows, that when by earthquake the sumit of a tower has been thrown down, it has slid off retaining its integrity — not separat-ing, but rubbing like a rock-slide. In the wide tracks, they

cultivate them — garden spots — very rich & loamy —
here fell the soldiers of Constantine — sowed in corruption & raised in potatoes. — These walls skirted by forrests of cemetery — the cypress growing thick as firs in a
Scotch plantation. Very old — a primal look — weird.
The walls seem the inexorable bar between the mansions
of the living & the dungeons of the dead. — Outside the
wall here is a Greek Church (for name see G.B. [Guide
Book]) Very beautiful, new upon an ancient site. (The
miraculous fish here) Decorated with banners of the virgin
& c. A beautiful cave chapel — a fountain of holy water
— Greeks come here & wash & burn a candle. All round
under the trees people smoking narguiles, drinking & eat-
ing, & riding. Gay crowds. Greek Sunday. Rode to the
wall-end at Sea of Marmara. The water dashes up against
the foundations here for 6 miles to the Seraglio. Went
into the Seven Towers. 200 feet high. 2 overthrown.
Immense thickness. Top of walls soil & sod. Like walking
on a terrace. Seven-sided enclosure, towers at angles.

Superb view of the city & sea. Dungeons — inscriptions. — Soldiers — A mosque. Immensely long ride back within the walls. Lonely streets. Passed under an arch of the acqueduct of Valens (?) In these lofty arches, ivied & weatherbeaten, & still grand, the ghost of Rome seems to stride with disdain of the hovels of this part of Stamboul. — Overtopping houses & trees &c. — Recrossed the 2d bridge to Pera. Too late for the Dancing Dervishes. Saw their convent. Reminded me of the Shakers. — Went towards the cemeteries of Pera. Great resort in summer evenings. Bank of the Bosphorus — like Brooklyn heights. From one point a superb view of Sea of Marmora & Princes Isles & Scutari. — *Armenian Funerals winding through the streets. Coffin covered with flowers born on a bier. Wax candles born on each side in daylight. Boys & men chanting alternately. Striking effect, winding through the narrow lanes.*— Saw a burial. Armenian. Juggling & incantations of the priests — making signs &c. — Nearby, saw a woman over a new grave — no grass on it yet. Such abandonment of misery!

Called to the dead, put her head down as close to it as possible; as if calling down a hatchway or celler; besought — "Why don't you speak to me? My God! — It is I! — Ah, speak — but one word!" — All deaf. — So much for consolation. — This woman & her cries haunt me horribly. *Street sights.* — The beauty of the human countenance. Among the women ugly faces rare. — Singular these races so exceed ours in this respect. Out of every other window look faces (Jew, Greek Armenian) which in England or America would be a cynosure in a ball room. — Wretched looking houses & filthy streets. *Tokens of pauperism without the paupers.* Out of old shanties peep lovely girls like lillies & *roses* growing in *cracked flower-pots.* Very shy & coy looking. Many houses walled. Lower story no windows. Great gates like fortresses. Sign of barberians. Robbers. Lattices to Turkish houses — little windows. Confusion of the streets — no leading one. No clue. Hopelessly lost. — Immense loads carried by porters. — Camels, donkeys mules, horses, & c.

—— These Constantinople bridges exceed London bridges for picturesqueness. Contrast between London Bridge & these. Kayacks darting under the wooden arches. Spread about like swarm of ants, when their hill is invaded. On either side rows of Turkish craft of uniform build & height, stand like troops presenting arms. Masts of black English steamers. Guide boys on the bridge. Greeks. beautiful faces. Lively, loquacious. Never wearied leaning over the balustrade & talking with them. —— Viewed from bridge, the great mosques are shown to be built most judiciously on the domed hills of the city. Fine effect. Seems a spreading, still further, of the tent.

Monday Dec 15. Utterly used up last night. This morning felt as if broken on the wheel. —— At eleven o'clock went out without guide. Mounted the Genoese tower. A prodigious structure. 60 feet in diameter. 200 or more high. Walls 12 feet thick. Stair in wall instead of at the tower's axis. Peculiar plan of the stairs. "Bakshesh." Terminates in a funnel-shaped affair, like a minaret. The highest loft nest of pigeons. From the gallery without, all round, another glorious view. (Three great views of Constantinople) All important to one desirous to learn something of the bearings of Pera &c. After much study succeeded in understanding the way to the two great bridges. Came down, & crossed the first bridge. There took a boy-guide to the bazar. (All the way from the G. Tower down steep hill to bridge, a steady stream of people) Immense crowds on the Constantinople side. Way led up steps into large court surrounding mosque. There clothes bazar, most busy scene; all the way to the Bazar by this route — crowds, crowds, crowds — *From the Fez caps, the way seemed paved with tiles.* — The Bazarr is formed of countless narrow aisles, overarched; and along the sides looks like rows of show-cases, a sort of sofa-counter before them (where lady customers recline) and a man in each. Persian bazzarr, superb. Pawnbrokers here, money changers, fellows with a bushel or two of coins of all nations, handling there change like

peddlers of nuts. — Rug merchants, (Angora wool) P. £
10 for small one. — After dismissing my boy, was followed for two or three hours by an infernal Greek, &
confederates. Dogged me; in & out & through the Bazaar.
I Could neither intimidate or elude them. Began to feel
nervous; remembered that much of the fearful interest of
Schiller's Ghost-Seer hangs upon being followed in Venice
by an Armenian. The mere mysterious, persistant, silent
following. At last escaped them. Went to the Aga Janissary's. Tower of Fire Watchman. An immense column of
the Saracenic order. Colossal Saracens. Saw drill of Turk
troops here. Disciplining the Tartarians. — Looked at the
burnt Column again. Base bedded in humus. It leans, is
split & chipped & cracked. Of a smoky purple color. Is
garlanded round with laurel (chisseled) at distances. (Cro-
ton water pipes on end) — Street scenes. Gilded carriages
of styles of Hogarths carriages. *Yellow boots daintily worn by*
the ladies in the mud — Intricacy of the place. No way to
get along the water-side — but by labyrinths of back

lanes. — Strange books in the *Mosque bazaar.* — English-
man at dinner. Invited me to Buyakderre — give me a
shake down & c. Said nothing would tempt him to go by
night through Galata. Assassinations every night. — His
cottage on Bospherus attacked by robbers. & c.

Tuesday Dec 16th At 8 1/2 A.M. took steamer up the
Bospherous to Buyukdereh. — Magnificent! The whole
scene one pomp of art & nature. Europe & Asia here
show their best. A challenge of contrasts, where by the
successively alternate sweeps of the shores both sides seem
to retire from every new proffer of beauty, again in some
grand prudery to advance with a bolder bid, and there-
upon again & again retiring, neither willing to retreat from
the contest of beauty. — Myrtle, Cypress, Cedar — ever-
greens. — The water clear as Ontario — the banks natural quays, shelving off like those of a canal. Large vessels
go close along shore. — The palaces of the Sultan —
the pleasure-houses — palaces of embassadors — The

white foam breaks on these white steps as on long lines of coral reefs. One peculiarity is the introduction of ocean into inland recesses. Ships anchor at the foot of ravines, deep among green basins, where the only canvass you would look for would be tents. — A gallery of ports & harbors, formed by the interchange of promontory & bay. Many parts like the Highlands of the Hudson, magnified. Porpoises sport in the blue; & large flights of pigeons overhead go through evolutions like those of armies. The sun shining on the palaces. View from the heights of Buuydereh. "Royal Albert" Euxine in sight from Buuyck-dereh. A chain of Lake Georges. No wonder the Czars have always coveted the capital of the Sultans. No wonder the Russian among his firs sighs for these myrtles. — Cedar & Cypress the only trees about the capital. — The Cypress a green minaret, & blends with the stone ones. Minaret (perhaps) derived from cypress shape. The inter-mingling of the dark tree with the bright spire expressive of the intermingling of life & death. — Holyday aspect of the Bospherus — The daisies are tipped with a crimson dawn, the very soil from [which] they spring has a ruddy hue. — Kiosks & fountains. One is amazed to see such delicate & fairy-like structures out of doors. One would think the elements would visit them too rudely; that they would melt away like castle of confectionary. Profuse sculpture & gilding & painting. — The bays sweep round in great ampitheatres. — Coming back from Bospherus, stood on the First Bridge Curious to stand amid these millions of fellow beings, some of whom seem not unwilling to accept our civilization, but with one consent rejecting much of our morality & all of our religion. Aspect of the Bridge like that of a Grand Fancy Ball. (An immense Persian Rug.) 1500000 men the actors. Banvard should paint a few hundred miles of this pageant of moving procession. Pedlers of all sorts & hawkers. Confectionery carried on head. A *chain of malefactors with iron rings about their necks — Indian file.* Porters immense burdens, brains doing the office of sinews. Others carrying burdens with poles, hands resting on each others shoulders. Military officers followed by running footmen. Ladies in yellow slippers. "Arabas." *Horses, whose docility & gentleness is much as harmless as any other foot passengers.* — Taking toll on the bridge (Three or four men) Splendid barges of the Pashas darting under the arches. A gentleman followed by his Greek servants on horseback. An officer conversing with his confidential — Wandered about in vicinity of Hippodrome till nearly dusk; lost myself, & finally came out at a gate on the Sea of Marmora. Returned to Tophanna by kayack. Interesting appearance of the walls here. Owing to the height of the shore above the sea, the fortifications here present a wall on the water side, but only a parapet on the land. Hence, from the sea, the houses look immensely lofty; they are of all shapes; in some parts their windows are formed by the open spaces of the battlements. In some parts, there are balconies. Several gates & archways are to be seen walled up. Collonades are disclosed, closed up. Pilasters. The fall, or rather crumbling away of the wall at one angle discloses a solitary column of white marble, looking strange as the resurrection of a body masoned up in a tomb. Reminded me of the Abbotsford walls — only, on a grand scale. Where huge masses of the masonry have fallen, they look like rocks, in confused heaps, the mortar as hard as the tile & stone. — At dinner to day the French attache estimated the population of Constantinople, suburbs, & banks of Bospherous at 1,500,000. A moderate estimate, judging from the swarms. — The fortress of Mamud II on Bospherous built in the likeness of the Arabic letters of his name. Conveys an idea of his spirit. Plenty who with a flourish skate their names on ice, but few who solidly build them up in walls upon the enduring rocks. — Extraordinary aspect of this fortress from the sea.

Wednesday Dec 17 Spent the day revisiting the Seraglio & c. — Owing to its peculair form St. Sophia viewed near to, looks as partly underground; as if you saw but the

superstructure of some immense temple, yet to be disin-
terred. You step *down* to enter. The dome has a kind of
dented appearance. like crown of old hat. Must
inevitably cave in one of these days. Within dome has
appearance (from its flatness) of an immense sounding
board. A firmament of masonry. The interior a positive
appropriation of space. The precious marbles of the interior. The worshipping — head prostration. — In the
part of the town near Old Seraglio — silent appearance
of the streets. Strange houses. Rows of quaint old side-
boards, cupboards, beauforts, tall Nuremberg clocks.
Lanes & allies of them. Seraglio. Many prohibited spots.
The Seraglio (proper) seems to be a quadrangle, on the
hill, where buildings present blank walls, buttressed, outside; but within open. Cypress overpeer the walls in
some parts. Grand view from Seraglio Point —
Marmora, Bospherus, Seutari. — The courts & grounds
of Seraglio have a strange, enchanted sort of look. —
The dogs. Roam about in bands like prairie wolves. No

masters. No Turk seems to have a dog. None domesticated. Nomadic. Against religion to kill them. Scavengers of the city. Terrible outcries at times. At night. Fighting of the dogs. Strange to come upon pack of them in some lonely lane. Mostly yellow, with long sharp noses. Some much scarred, others mangey. See them lying amidst refuse, hardly tell them from it. — Same color. See them over a dead horse on the beach. — Wandering about came across Black Hole in the street. Did not enter far. — Harem (sacred) on board steam boats. Lattice division. Ladies pale, straight noses, regular features, fine busts. Look like nuns in their plain dress, but with a roundness of bust not belonging to that character. Perfect decorum between sexes. No ogling. No pertness. No looking for admiration. Cyprians. No drunkards. Saw not a single one, though liqour is sold. — Industry. — Beauty of fountain near St. Sophia. Gilding. Grapes & Foliage.

Thursday Dec 18   In morning took caique, & crossed the Bospherus to Scutari. Luxurious sailing. Cushioned like ottoman. You lie in the boat's bottom. Body beneath the surface. A boat bed. Kaick a sort of carved trencher or tray. — Fleet of fishermen at mouth of Golden Horn. Calm of water. Tide-rips. Sun shining on Sultan's Palaces. Sunrise opposite the Seraglio. *As Constantinople is finest site for capital, so Seraglio for pleasure-grounds, in the world.* — Great barracks at Scutari. Noble view of Constantinople & up Bospherous. Cemeteries like Black Forrest. Thuringian look. Roads passing through it. Beautiful daisies. The quays. The water mosque. The hills & beach. — *General thoughts about Constantinople.* As for its mud, mere wet pollen of a flower. —Tenedos Wine on table — The Negro Mussleman. Unlike other dispersed nations (Jews, Armenians, Gypsies) who proof against proselytism adhere to the faith first delivered to their fathers. Negro is indifferent to forms as horse to caparisons. — At 4 P.M. sailed in steamer Acadia for Alexandria, via Smyrna. It was sunset

ere we rounded Seraglio Point. Glorious sight. Scutari &
its heights, glowed like sapphire. Wonderful clearness of
air. As a promontory is covered with trees, terraced up
clear to its top, so Constantinople with houses. Long line
of walls. — Out into Sea of Marmora.

Gülten Akin

SONG OF A DWELLER IN A HIGH-RISE BLOCK

They piled the houses high,
in front long balconies.
Far below was water
far below were trees

---

*Gülten Akin's sharp portraits of modern Istanbul have established her as one
of Turkey's brightest poets. She was born in Istanbul in 1933 and has gone
on to produce numerous mini-masterpieces, including "Song to an Ageless
Woman," "Laughing Stock," and "Song of a Dweller in a High-Rise Block."
Many of her poems were collected in the 1992 volume* Modern Turkish
Poetry.

They piled the houses high,
a thousand stairs to climb.
The outlook a far cry
and friendships further still.

They piled the houses high
in glass and concrete drowned.
In our wisdom we forgot
the earth that was remote
and those who stayed earthbound.

Michael Palin

ISTANBUL

WOKEN BY THE distorted sound of a pre-recorded muezzin calling the faithful to prayer. It's 5:30. Breakfast of orange juice, cereal and honeycomb—things I have not seen since Helsinki, three weeks ago. Fraser has had a nightmare in which he had to wire every minaret in Istanbul for sound.

Istanbul is a very noisy city, much of the noise from a huge construction programme. A companion to

Michael Palin was one of the cofounders of the BBC Television series Monty Python's Flying Circus. *He has since moved on to more respectable ventures, including two amusing documentaries of his travels around the world. This is from the book version of his second trip,* Pole to Pole *(1993).*

the famously crowded Galata Bridge across the Golden Horn is almost complete. A last massive section of its six-lane highway, waiting to be lowered into position, rears up at a right angle, a huge phallic symbol of regeneration. Sevim says the reconstruction is going on at such a pace that her husband, given a month's notice of redevelopment, went in to work one Monday morning to find his shop had gone. There are those with reservations about the pace of change. One is Altemur Kilic, a Turkish writer, diplomat and friend of Turgut Ozal, the President. He remembers Istanbul only 30 years ago as a city of 750,000 people, home to a flourishing number of foreign communities—Greek, Jewish, Armenian and what was known as the Levantine, comprising Italians, English and French who had lived in Turkey all their lives. He himself went to the English-run Istanbul High School for Boys whose headmaster, Mr. Peach, he knew affectionately as Baba, "Father." The teachers caned him regularly. He smiles happily at the memory. "My father authorized

them to do so. It helped my character." In between can-
ings Altemur played cricket, read the *Boy's Own Paper* and
grew up in an Istanbul which was small enough to give
him "a sense of being somebody in a big city." Now the
city population has swelled to 8 million and the real
Istanbuliots, as he calls them, are very few.

As I step out of his elegant, unostentatious house
on a small sloping street in Emirgan, I could be in the
South of France, with the blue waters of the Bosporus
catching the sunlight, people taking a drink or a coffee
beneath the shade of ash and mimosa trees and the almost
unbroken line of passing traffic.

Down by the Galata Bridge, close by the old
spice markets, the pace of Istanbul life is at its most fre-
netic. Ferries are constantly loading and unloading provid-
ing a regular and copious passing trade for the street food
sellers. Fishermen dart in, light up charcoal braziers and
rocking crazily in the wash of the ferries sell their grilled
catch then and there. You could have a street dinner every

night of the week here and never eat the same menu twice. Apart from the fish, served in luscious sandwiches of hot fresh bread, tomato and onion, there are kebabs, pretzels, walnuts, pancakes and stuffed mussels, corn on the cob, succulent slices of melon and as much sweet tea as you can drink.

Back in England, it's the first day of the football season and in my hotel the new BBC World Service Television is showing Episode 5 of *Around the World in 80 Days.*

THE CREW ARE up early to shoot the sunrise from the top of the 600-year-old Galata Tower, where in May 1453, the Genoese Christians handed over control of the city to the Ottoman Muslims, a key moment in European history. It is at breakfast at the Pera Palas Hotel that I hear the first news of modern history in the making. Those with short-wave radios have heard word from the Soviet Union that Gorbachev has been overthrown in a right-wing coup. Nothing more is known at the moment.

I think of all the friends we made—Irena and Volodya and Edward and Sasha and the Lenin impersonator, and I know that if the news is true things can only be worse for them. Selfishly, we can only be thankful for our extraordinarily lucky escape. If this had happened three days earlier, the *Junost* may never have left Odessa and we would have been stranded. If it had happened three *weeks* earlier we would never have been allowed into the Soviet Union.

The shadow of this great event hangs over the city, giving everything else we do a certain air of unreality. Some of the unreality is there already, especially in Room 411 of the Pera Palas Hotel. This is the room in which Agatha Christie wrote *Murder on the Orient Express.* It's small and rather cramped and you wouldn't get much writing done nowadays as they've just built an eight-lane highway below the window. After Agatha Christie died in 1976, Warner Brothers wanted to make a film about the mystery of 11 lost days of her life. An American medium, one Tamara Rand, said that in a trance she had seen an hotel in Istanbul and in Room 411 of this hotel she had seen Agatha Christie hiding the key to her diary under the floorboards. On 7 March 1979, the room was searched and a rusty key was found. The president of the hotel company, sensing Warner Brothers' interest but miscalculating their generosity, put the key in a safe demanding 2 million dollars, plus 15 percent of the film's profits. Here the key remains. Its age has been authenticated and as Agatha Christie was highly secretive about travel arrangements it's considered unlikely that the medium can have known about the Pera Palas before she saw it in her trance.

It makes 411 rather a creepy place and I'm glad to get out and into the bustle of Pera Street—the mile-long main thoroughfare of Istanbul. The best way to see it is from one of the venerable red and cream trams that run its length, though I must confess I do catch breath when I notice the number of the tram we're on—411.

I buy a Panama hat for under £6 off an elderly French-speaking Turk at a shop by the tram stop. I'm not keen on hats but with the weather getting hotter by the day, I can see the advantages.

As a result of climate, history and geographical position, Istanbul is the quintessential trading city. Russia and the Mediterranean and Europe and Asia meet here, and though a walk through the endless arcades of the old covered market gives an overwhelming sense of richness and variety, there is no better place to see trade in its rawest, purest form than the square outside the gates of the Beyazit II Mosque and the impressive Islamic-arched entrance of Istanbul University. Here an extraordinary dance of commerce goes on. Groups are constantly gathering, splitting and reforming. Eyes are always on the move. These are furtive people on the very edge of the law, buying and selling in the spirit, if not the currency, of this great commercial city. There are Azerbaijanis, Iranians, Poles, Romanians, Ukrainians and Afghans. Most of them sell out of black plastic bags. I see Marlboro cigarettes traded for dollars and plastic train sets, cheap Eastern European trainers, an anorak, some metal ornaments—all attracting the crowds.

By the end of this hot, hard day the ministrations of a proper Turkish bath, a hammam, are irresistible.

The Cagaloglu Hammam, a splendid emporium of cleanliness, is this year celebrating 300 years in business, during which time it has cleaned, among others, King Edward VII, Kaiser Wilhelm, Florence Nightingale and Tony Curtis. I can choose from a "self-service bath,"—the cheapest option, a "scrubbed assisted bath," a "Massage à la Turk—you'll feel years younger after this vigorous revitalizing treatment" or the "Sultan Service," which promises, modestly, that "you will feel reborn." At 120,000 Turkish lira, about £17, rebirth seems a snip and after signing up, I'm given a red and white check towel and shown to a small changing cubicle. Through the glass I can see a group of masseurs with long droopy mustaches, hairy chests, bulbous stomachs and an occasional tattoo. At that moment a Turkish father and son emerge from a cubicle and the little boy, who looks to be only eight or nine, is ushered toward the steam room by one of these desperadoes with a reassuring gentleness and good humor.

The steam room, the hararet, is set to one side of an enormous central chamber with walls and floor of silver-grey marble, and a dome supported by elegant columns and arches. Whilst I work up a good dripping sweat from the underfloor heating I get talking to a fellow bather, an Italian. He has driven to Istanbul from Bologna, and had come quite unscathed through Yugoslavia, where there is a state of civil war, but had found newly-liberated Romania a dark and dangerous place. Gasoline was almost unavailable. He bought a can which he found later to be water. I asked him if there was any more news from the USSR. He said he had heard that Leningrad had been sealed off and tanks had moved into the Kremlin.

Then it's my turn on the broad inlaid marble massage slab called the Gobek Tasi. I'm rubbed, stretched and at one point mounted and pulled up by my arms before being taken off and soaped all over by a masseur who keeps saying "Good?," in a tone which brooks no disagreement. He dons a sinister black glove the size of a baseball mitt. (The brochure describes it as "a handknitted Oriental washing cloth," but it feels like a Brillo pad.) Never have I been so thoroughly scoured. The dirt and skin rolled off me like the deposits from a school rubber. How can I have been so filthy and not known about it?

There is a small bar giving on to an open court-yard at the back of the Hammam. Sitting here with a glass of raki and a bowl of grapes luxuriating in the after-glow of the bath at the end of a long day, I feel as content as I ever could.

Lady Mary Wortley Montagu

EMBASSY TO CONSTANTINOPLE

To Lady Mar—
Adrianople April 1, 1717

I WISH TO God (dear sister) that you was as regular in letting me have the pleasure of knowing what passes on your side of the globe as I am careful in endeavoring to amuse you by the account of all I see that I think you

---

In 1716, Lady Mary Wortley Montagu followed her husband, an ambassador, from their cozy London flat to the wilds of Turkey. This is notable, since proper women simply did not travel in eighteenth-century England. The scandal Montagu caused was only heightened when she took to donning native Turkish robes. This excerpt is from her journals.

care to hear of. You content yourself with telling me over and over that the town is very dull. It may possibly be dull to you when every day does not present you with something new, but for me that am in arrear at least two months' news, all that seems very stale with you would be fresh and sweet here; pray let me into more particulars. I will try to awaken your gratitude by giving you a full and true relation of the novelties of this place, none of which would surprise you more than a sight of my person as I am now in my Turkish habit, though I believe you would be of my opinion that 'tis admirably becoming. I intend to send you my picture; in the meantime accept of it here.

The first piece of my dress is a pair of drawers, very full, that reach to my shoes and conceal the legs more modestly than your petticoats. They are of a thin, rose-colour damask brocaded with silver flowers, my shoes of white kid leather embroidered with gold. Over this hands my smock of a fine white silk gauze edged with embroidery. This smock has wide sleeves hanging half-way down the arm and is closed at the neck with a diamond button, but the shape and color of the bosom very well to be distinguished through it. The *antery* is a waistcoat made close to the shape, of white and gold damask, with very long sleeves falling back and fringed with deep gold fringe, and should have diamond or pearl buttons. My *caftan* of the same stuff with my drawers is a robe exactly fitted to my shape and reaching to my feet, with very long straight falling sleeves. Over this is the girdle of about four fingers broad, which all that can afford have entirely of diamonds or other precious stones. Those that will not be at the expense have it of exquisite embroidery on satin, but it must be fastened before with a clasp of diamonds. The *curdee* is a loose robe they throw off or put on according to the weather, being of a rich brocade (mine is green and gold) either lined with ermine or sables; the sleeves reach very little below the shoulders. The head-dress is composed of a cap called *talpack,* which is in winter of fine velvet embroidered with pearls or diamonds and in summer of a light, shining silver stuff. This is fixed on one side of the head, hanging a little way down with a gold tassel and bound on either side with a circle of diamonds (as I have seen several) or a rich embroidered handkerchief. On the other side of the head the hair is laid flat, and here the ladies are at liberty to show their fancies, some putting flowers, others a plume of heron's feathers, and in short what they please, but the most general fashion is a large bouquet of jewels made like natural flowers, that is the buds of pearl, the roses of different coloured rubies, the jasmines of diamonds, jonquils of topazes, etc., so well set and enamelled 'tis hard to imagine anything of that kind so beautiful. The hair hangs at its full length behind, divided into tresses braided with pearl or riband, which is always in great quantity.

I never saw in my life so many fine heads of hair. I have counted one hundred and ten of these tresses of one lady's, all natural; but it must be owned that every beauty is more common here than with us. 'Tis surpris-

ing to see a young woman that is not very handsome.
They have naturally the most beautiful complexions in
the world and generally large black eyes. I can assure you
with great truth that the Court of England (though I
believe it the fairest in Christendom) cannot show so
many beauties as are under our protection here. They
generally shape their eyebrows, and the Greeks and Turks
have a custom of putting round their eyes on the inside a
black tincture that, at a distance or by candlelight, adds
very much to the blackness of them. I fancy many of our
ladies would be overjoyed to know this secret, but 'tis
too visible by day. They dye their nails rose colour; I
own I cannot enough accustom myself to this fashion to
find any beauty in it.

As to their morality or good conduct, I can say
like Harlequin, "'Tis just as 'tis with you"; and the
Turkish ladies don't commit one sin the less for not
being Christians. Now I am a little acquainted with their
ways, I cannot forbear admiring either the exemplary dis-

cretion or extreme stupidity of all the writers that have given accounts of 'em. 'Tis very easy to see they have more liberty than we have, no woman of what rank soever being permitted to go in the streets without two muslins, one that covers her face all but her eyes and another that hides the whole dress of her head and hangs half-way down her back; and their shapes are wholly concealed by a thing they call a *ferigée,* which no woman of any sort appears without. This has strait sleeves that reach to their fingers' ends and it laps all round 'em, not unlike a riding hood. In winter 'tis of cloth, and in summer, plain stuff or silk. You may guess how effectually this disguises them, that there is no distinguishing the great lady from her slave, and 'tis impossible for the most jealous husband to know his wife when he meets her, and no man dare either touch or follow a woman in the street.

This perpetual masquerade gives them entire liberty of following their inclinations without danger of discovery. The most usual method of intrigue is to send an appointment to the lover to meet the lady at a Jew's shop, which are as notoriously convenient as our Indian houses, and yet even those that don't make that use of 'em do not scruple to go and buy penn'orths and tumble over rich goods, which are chiefly to be found amongst that sort of people. The great ladies seldom let their gallants know who they are, and 'tis so difficult to find it out that they can very seldom guess at her name they have corresponded with above half a year together. You may easily imagine the number of faithful wives very small in a country where they have nothing to fear from their lovers' indiscretion, since we see so many that have the courage to expose themselves to that in this world and all the threatened punishment of the next, which is never preached to the Turkish damsels. Neither have they much to apprehend from the resentment of their husbands, those ladies that are rich having all their money in their own hands, which they take with 'em upon a divorce with an addition which he is obliged to give 'em. Upon the whole, I look upon the Turkish women as the only free people in the empire. The very Divan pays a respect to 'em, and the Grand Signior himself, when a Pasha is executed, never violates the privilege of the harem (or women's apartment) which remains unsearched entire to the widow. They are queens of their slaves, which the husband has no permission so much as to look upon, except it be an old woman or two that his lady chooses. 'Tis true their law permits them four wives, but there is no instance of a man of quality that makes use of this liberty, or of a woman of rank that would suffer it. When a husband happens to be inconstant (as those things will happen) he keeps his mistress in a house apart and visits her as privately as he can, just as 'tis with you. Amongst all the great men here I only know the *defterdar* (i.e., treasurer) that keeps a number of she slaves for his own use (that is, on his own side of the house, for a slave once given to serve a lady is entirely at her disposal), and he is spoke of as a libertine, or what we should call a rake, and his wife won't see him, though she continues to live in his house.

Thus you see, dear sister, the manners of mankind do not differ so widely as our voyage writers would make us believe. Perhaps it would be more entertaining to add a few surprising customs of my own invention, but nothing seems to me so agreeable as truth, and I believe nothing so acceptable to you. I conclude with repeating the great truth of my being, dear sister, etc.

Anonymous

WHAT HAPPENED TO HADJI

HADJI WAS A merchant in the Great Bazaar of Stambul. Being a pious Mohammedan, he was of course a married man, but even so he was not invulnerable to the charms of women. It happened one day that a charming hanum came to his shop to purchase some spices. After the departure of his fair visitor, Hadji, do what he might, could not drive her image from his mind's eye. Furthermore, he was greatly puzzled by a tiny black bag

---

The Anonymous author of "What Happened to Hadji" penned this wry classic in the 1600s. The brief story has grown to be a staple of Turkish folklore.

containing twelve grains of wheat, which the hanum had evidently forgotten.

Till a late hour that night did Hadji remain in his shop, in the hope that either the hanum or one of her servants would come for the bag and thus give him the means of seeing her again, or at least of learning where she lived. But Hadji was doomed to disappointment, and, much preoccupied, he returned to his house. There he sat, plunged in thought, unresponsive to his wife's conversation.

Hadji remained downcast day after day, but at last, giving way to his wife's entreaties, he told what had happened and admitted that ever since that fatal day his soul had been in bondage to the fair unknown.

"Oh, husband," replied his wife, "and do you not understand what that black bag containing the twelve grains of wheat means?"

"Alas, no," replied Hadji.

"Why, my husband, it is plain; plain as if it had

been told. She lives in the Wheat Market, at house number 12, with a black door."

Much excited, Hadji rushed off and found that there was a number 12 in the Wheat Market, with a black door, so he promptly knocked. The door opened, and whom should he behold but the lady in question! Instead of speaking to him, however, she threw a basin of water out into the street and then shut the door. Hadji did not know what to think of this. Having lingered about the doorway for a time, he at length returned home. He greeted his wife more pleasantly than he had done for many days and told her of his adventure.

"Why," said his wife, "don't you understand what the basin of water thrown out of the door means?"

"Alas, no," said Hadji.

"Veyh! Veyh!" she exclaimed pityingly, "it means that at the back of the house there is a running stream, and that you must go to her that way."

Off rushed Hadji, and found that his wife was

right; there *was* a running stream at the back of the house, so he knocked at the back door. The hanum, however, instead of opening it, came to the window, showed a mirror, reversed it, and then disappeared. Hadji lingered at the back of the house for a long time, but, seeing no further sign of life, he returned to his own home much dejected. On his entering the doorway, his wife greeted him with, "Well, was it not as I told you?"

"Yes," said Hadji. "You are truly a wonderful woman! But I do not know why she came to the window and showed me a mirror, both front and back, instead of opening the door."

"Oh," said his wife, "that is very simple; she means that you must go when the face of the moon has reversed itself—about ten o'clock." The hour arrived. Hadji hurried off, and so did his wife; the one to see his love, and the other to inform the police.

Whilst Hadji and his charmer were talking in the garden the police seized them and carried them both off to prison; and Hadji's wife, having accomplished her mission, returned home.

The next morning she baked a quantity of *lokma* cakes, and, taking them to the prison, begged entrance of the guards, and permission to distribute those cakes to the prisoners, for the repose of the souls of her dead. This being a request which could not be denied, she was allowed to enter. Finding the cell in which the lady who had attracted her husband was confined, she offered to save her the disgrace of exposure, provided she would consent never again to cast loving eyes on Hadji the merchant. Those conditions were gratefully accepted, and Hadji's wife changed places with the prisoner.

When they were brought before the judge, Hadji was thunderstruck to see his wife, but, being a wise man, he held his peace and let her do the talking, which she did most vigorously. Vehemently did she protest against the insult inflicted on both her and her husband. What right had the police to bring them to prison because they chose to converse in a garden, seeing that they were lawfully wedded people? To witness that they were man and wife she called upon the watchman and the priest of the district and several of her neighbors.

Poor Hadji was dumbfounded, as, accompanied by his wife, he soon after left the prison where he had expected to stay at least a year or two. "Truly though art a wonderful woman!" was all he was able to say.

Alev Lytle Croutier

HAREM

I WAS BORN in a *konak* (old house), which once was the harem of a pasha. During my childhood, servants and odalisques lived there with us. I grew up in Turkey, listening to stories and songs that could easily have come from the *One Thousand and One Nights.* People around me often whispered things about harems; my own grandmother and her sister had been brought up in one. Since

---

Alev Lytle Croutier's rollicking account of the Topkapi Palace harems was published in 1989. The book, Harem, *ranges from her growing up in Turkey to the surprising place of women in Turkish society—then and now.*

then, I have come to see that these were not ordinary stories. But for me, as a child, they were, for I had not yet known any others.

My paternal grandmother, Zehra, was the first person from whom I heard the word *harem* and who made allusions to harem life. She was the daughter of a wealthy gunpowder maker in Macedonia. As was the custom until the twentieth century, she and her sisters had been brought up in a "harem," or a separate part of a house where women were isolated; the only men they encountered were their blood relatives. On rare occasions they went out, always heavily veiled. Sometimes silk tunnels were stretched from the door of the house to a carriage, so that the women could leave without being seen from the street. Their marriages had already been arranged by the family. None of them saw their husbands until their wedding day. Then they moved to his house, to live together with their mother-in-law and his other women relatives.

My grandmother married my grandfather when she was fourteen. He was forty and her father's best friend. She was a simple, uneducated girl. He was a respected scholar. Ten years later, she was widowed. With one of her sisters, she moved into her brother-in-law's harem; and there the two sisters brought their children up together, as one family.

Threatened by the Balkan Wars, they left everything behind in Macedonia, including their parents, and fled to Anatolia. They sought refuge and settled down in Istanbul in 1906. They were among the last women who had lived in harems; in 1909, with the fall of Abdulhamid, harems were abolished and declared unlawful.

I do not remember very much of the house in Izmir (Smyrna) where I was born. It faced the sea, was five stories high, and it had a *hamam* (bath house) where groups of women came to bathe. A giant granite rock behind the house isolated it from the world. It was said that before us, an old pasha, his two wives, and other women occupied the place. As a child, I played dress-up with embroidered clothes that the women from another era had left behind.

In 1950, with my parents and grandmother, I moved to an apartment house in Ankara that was inhabited by assorted family members. We lived as an extended family—two uncles, three aunts, my grandmother, my great-aunt, many cousins, and *odalisques* (servant girls) who were gifts from my great-uncle, Faik Pasha, and owned by the family. He had found them in a cave after their parents had been killed in a border dispute near Iran. The Ottoman palaces were gone, but not the need to live as one big family: clustered apartments were occupied by large families.

When the women gathered together, the old sisters told stories and argued about facts and details, occasionally agreeing on some. We all participated in rituals, vanishing rites the sisters had transported from their harem days. We learned to make concoctions to remove hair, brew good coffee, distribute a sacrificed sheep's entrails to the poor, cast spells, and give the evil eye to protect ourselves. These were the origins of my exposure to harem life, accepted as part of a prosaic existence.

When I was eighteen years old, I left Turkey and came to live in the United States. In 1978, fifteen years later, I returned to Istanbul to visit my family and sort out my impressions of my birthplace. I returned, carrying new baggage with me: an expatriate's eye and a self-conscious awareness of art history and of feminist rhetoric. It was not surprising, then, that I found myself fascinated with the recently opened harem apartments of Topkapi Palace—the Grand Seraglio, or the Sublime Porte, as it was known in the West. It had belonged to the *sultans* (emperors) of the Ottoman Dynasty, who had kept their women hidden away here from around 1540 through the early 1900s—four hundred years of life and culture. All that remained now of the thousands of women who had lived in these rooms, in fantastic luxury and isolation,

were their empty boudoirs, their echoing baths, and countless, impenetrable mysteries.

This visit to the harem of the Topkapi Palace
haunted me. I was obsessed with the notion that these
same stairways once felt the flying feet, these alleys, the
soft rustle of their garments. The walls seemed to whisper
secrets pleading to be heard. The marble floors of the
bath seemed to echo centuries of pouring water. Obviously, more was concealed here than the popular notion
of sensuality attached to the word *harem* and what I had
been exposed to as a child. It seemed as though I had
stepped into a unique and extraordinary reality—a cocoon
of women in their evolutionary cycle. Questions kept
insinuating themselves. What had happened here during
all these years? Who were these women? What did they
do from day to day?

I began searching in earnest for documents on
harems—books, letters, travelogues, paintings, pho-
tographs—to help reconstruct a candid image of this

veiled world. What I found were fragments—romanticized descriptions of the imperial harem by Western travelers, writers, and diplomats, a few smuggled letters and poems written by the women themselves, and tedious studies by historians whose primary interest was royal life and palace politics, not the uncounted, unnamed women of the harem.

Simultaneously I had to probe deeper into my own family history. When I expressed my need to find out everything about harems, on which nothing definitive had been written, many of my relatives and friends came forth. They helped me remember things. They showed me strange books and letters. They shared ephemeral stories, things that had happened a long time ago, so that I could write about them.

Physical and spiritual isolation of women, and polygamy, I discovered, were not unique to Turkey. Harems existed throughout history in different parts of the Asian world, known by different names, such as *purdah* ("curtain") in Indian and, in Persia, *enderun* or *zenane.* In China, the Forbidden City of Peking also had cloistered women and used eunuchs to protect and guard them. But the most highly and extensively developed harem was that of the Grand Seraglio. What happened there came to be seen as the paradigm of all harems.

In the Seraglio alone, thousands of women lived and died with only each other to know of their lives. By piecing together the fragments collected over the years, I hoped to discover this mysterious, beautiful, and unbelievably repressive world concealed for so many centuries behind the veil. What will these women tell us, about themselves and about ourselves?

HAREM OF THE SERAGLIO

THE TURKISH TRIBES, including the Ottomans, practiced polygamy prior to the conquest of the Byzantine capital, Constantinople, in 1453. Sultan Mehmed II, known to history as "the Conqueror," was obsessed with making his new metropolis, which he called Istanbul, a replica of Constantine's—only more opulent. He allowed the *valide sultana* (mother sultana) to organize her house as nearly as possible in the manner of the gynaecea (women's apartments) of Empress Helen, widow of Constantine. The gynaecea were situated in the remotest part of her palace, lying beyond an interior court; women lived here separately, divided into task groups. Mehmed himself adopted such Byzantine customs as the sequestering of royalty, establishing a palace school, and the keeping of household slaves. The Islamic practice of polygamy combined neatly with these Byzantine customs and resulted in the harem.

The early Ottoman sultans had married daughters of Anatolian governors and of the Byzantine royal family. After the conquest of Constantinople, it became customary to marry odalisques. The women in harems, except those born in it, came from all over Asia, Africa, and, occasionally, Europe.

According to ancient legend, the Seraglio Point, a magnificent isthmus extending between the Marmara Sea and the Golden Horn, was named by the Delphic Oracle as the best site for a new colony and became the Acropolis of ancient Byzantium. A decade after the conquest, Mehmed the Conqueror built Topkapi Palace—known in the West as the Grand Seraglio or the Sublime Porte—on the same sacred point.

In his poem "The Palace of Fortune" (1772), Sir William (Oriental) Jones invokes a palace of such opulence:

> In mazy curls the flowing jasper wav'd
> O'er its smooth bed with polish'd agate pav'd;
> And on a rock of ice, by magick rais'd,
> High in the midst a gorgeous palace blaz'd.

The Seraglio was the seat of imperial power, housing thousands of people involved in the sultan's personal and administrative service. The most private section, carefully separated from the rest of the palace, was the sultan's harem, which moved to the Seraglio for the first time in 1541, with Sultana Roxalena, and lasted until 1909. The ever-changing female family lived, loved, and died here for four centuries. It became the ultimate symbol, the quintessence of harem, the system of sequestering women.

The harem was located between the *Mabeyn* (Court)—the sultan's private apartments—and the apartments of the chief black eunuch. It had almost four hundred rooms centered around the Courtyard of the Valide Sultana, containing the apartments and dormitories of other women.

The Carriage House and the Bird House, which connected the harem to the outside world, were carefully guarded from within by the corps of eunuchs and, outside, by halberdiers, or royal guards. The Carriage House was the real entry to the harem; all contact with the outside was made through its gate, which opened at dawn and closed at dusk.

The eunuchs' quarters led into a courtyard, which opened on the right to the Golden Road, in the center to the valide sultana's quarters, and on the left to the apartments of the odalisques. The luxury of the living quarters depended on the status of the person occupying them. The sultan, of course, had the most magnificent accommodations. High-ranking women had private apartments. Novice odalisques and eunuchs lived in dormitories.

During the fifteenth and sixteenth centuries, the population of the harem dropped from over a thousand women to a few hundred, because the young princes were given governorships in various provinces and left the Seraglio, escorted by their own harems. After the seventeenth century, however, with reforms in the inheritance laws that allowed the princes to live in the palace with their own women—albeit as captives in the *Kafes* (the Golden Cage)—the harem population increased to almost two thousand.

At its zenith, the Ottoman Empire was enormous, stretching from the Caucasus Mountains to the Persian Gulf, from the Danube to the Nile. The history of the Seraglio and its harem symbolizes the fluctuating fortunes of the empire. The great expense of upkeep, the ruthless rivalry among the women, intrigues that influenced political affairs, and, ultimately, the exquisite beauty of these women of many nationalities fascinated the entire world. Everyone was curious to know what happened behind the harem walls—but no one was allowed behind them. Foreign ambassadors and artists reported accounts obtained from peddlers or servant women who had entered, but such narratives were often muddled by wishful exoticism. To this day, the reality is difficult to ascertain.

PIERRE LOTI

ON THE OTHER side of the Bosphorus from the Beylerbey Palace where the empress stayed, in the hills of

Eyub, overlooking the Golden Horn, is an open-air café called Café Pierre Loti. Here the famous author once lived, under an assumed identity as a Turkish bey. On many weekends, I went there with my friends. We sat under the century-old sycamores, sipping black tea served in samovars and digesting the view. What we saw were shipyards, paper factories, and enormous mountains of coal—no longer a "city of cut jasper," featuring the romantic vista of Sweet Waters with myriad colorful kayiks. But we still fantasized that city, Because Loti had evoked it so well for us in his novels.

Born into a Huguenot family as Julien Viaud, Loti joined the Navy as a young man, wanting to see the world. His voyages took him to the most exotic and far-off places; in each, Loti pursued rose-colored romance and wrote books about love affairs with beautiful women of strange cultures. Evocative and nostalgic, his novels speak of melancholy, disenchantment, incurable solitude, and death.

No place, however, enthralled him so much as Istanbul. It was love at first sight. He had found *his* subject and, with it, he formed a livelong love affair, producing two gems of Orientalist literature, *Aziyade* (1877) and *The Disenchanted* (1906). Loti lived what he wrote: "Behind those heavy iron bars, two large eyes were fixed on me. The eyebrows were drawn across so that they met. . . . A white veil was wound tightly around the head, leaving only the brow, and those great eyes free. They were green—that sea-green which poets of the Orient once sang." This was Aziyade, whose enigmatic and untouchable beauty consumed Loti. She was a Circassian kadin in the harem of a bey. Defying all danger, Loti's servant Samuel arranged a nocturnal rendezvous. They met on a boat:

> *Aziyade's barque is filled with soft rugs, cushions and Turkish coverlets—all the refinements and nonchalance of the Orient, so that it seems a floating bed, rather than a barque. . . . All dangers surround this bed of ours, which*

drifts slowly out to sea: it is as if two beings are united
there to taste the intoxicating pleasure of the impossible.

When we are far enough from all else, she holds
out her arms to me. I reach her side, trembling as I touch
her. At this first contact I am filled with mortal languor:
her veils are impregnated with all the perfumes of the Ori-
ent, her flesh is firm and cool.

The prose is purple, and the fantasy boundless.
Loti and Aziyade have many such nights of pleasure on
her boat. Finally, Loti's ship has to leave; the lovers part;
he promises to return. But he does not, and Aziyade dies
of a broken heart.

After Aziyade's death, heartbroken himself, Loti
did not return to Istanbul for almost twenty years. In
the meantime, it had become the West's turn to influence the East. Eastern women began learning foreign
languages and attending schools; by the turn of the century, though they still lived in harems, they were a new

breed, well-educated and outspoken, envious of European women's freedom, longing to shed their veils, show their faces, and even choose their own husbands.

Loti received a letter from such a woman, named Djénane, who entreated him to come to Istanbul. Beginning to age, tempted to see Aziyade's land once again, he decided to return. This was the beginning of a novel called *The Disenchanted*.

Djénane and two accomplices arranged clandestine meetings with Loti in the most exotic and romantic parts of Istanbul. The women filled him with heartbreaking accounts of their miserable lives, in the hope of persuading Loti to write a novel about the suffering of women still living in harems. The novelist was less interested in politics than in romance, so the women fabricated a tale straight out of *One Thousand and One Nights*. What they had failed to anticipate was his falling in love with Djénane, and how such an affair would place all their lives in peril. To make Loti leave Istanbul, they staged a fake funeral, pretending Djénane, like Aziyade, had died of a heart broken by forbidden love.

Loti returned to Paris and wrote *The Disenchanted* (1906).

But the story does not end here. Soon after the writer's departure, the women on whom the book was based also fled to Paris, where they became a *cause célèbre*, appearing at the most exclusive parties. They were written about, painted, and sculpted by the greatest artists of the era, among them Henri Rousseau and August Rodin. Moreover, after Loti's death, a French woman named Madame Lera, who wrote under the pseudonym Marc Helys, published *Le Secret des désenchantées*, which purported to reveal that she herself had posed as Djénane with the help of her two Turkish friends; the three women had simply wanted to amuse themselves with Loti. Marc Helys's "revelation" was challenged, but no one knows for sure whether she was writing fiction or reporting fact.

EMANCIPATION OF THE EAST

THE PUBLICATION OF *The Disenchanted* not only stirred up scandal, it brought the suffragettes to the rescue. Turkey was suddenly flooded with European women who were appalled at the situation of their sisters, still living under such submission. They set out on a crusade to free these unfortunates. Eastern women had always held an interest for European feminists. Sir Richard Burton's wife, Isabelle, would deliberately appear in low-cut dresses during social gatherings to set a provocative example, and in Lebanon, at an embassy reception, she had the wives sit in chairs and ordered their husbands to serve them tea and cakes.

In Turkey, the inevitable uprising of women was under way by the turn of the century. The social upheaval so threatened the established order that in 1901 Sultan Abdul Hamid II issued an edict prohibiting the employment of Christian teachers in harems, the education of Turkish children in foreign schools, and the appearance in public of Turkish women with foreign women. These restrictions only served to force the issue among women, who rebelled by secretly meeting and organizing. Messages were carried from harem to harem—protected by the certainty that Moslem women are never searched. The "Young Turks," idealistic poets and intellectuals, expressed their own feelings of shame about perpetuating polygamy. Faced with the stark reality of a diseased empire, they shed their intellectual idealism and began mobilizing in Macedonia. In 1909, they overthrew the sultan and established a constitutional government. It would take another decade for major changes actually to become effective in Turkish society, but by the 1920s women became fully integrated into public life. The revolutionary leader Kemal Atatürk challenged: "Is it possible that, while one half of a community stays chained to the ground, the other half can rise to the skies? There is no question—the steps of progress must be taken to accomplish the various stages of the journey into the land of progress and renovation. If this is done, our revolution will be successful."

Veils came off. The massive layers of clothing were shed and, with them, the years of suppression and isolation. Harems were declared unlawful; polygamy abolished.

THE LAST PICTURE

ONE OF THE most touching and strange scenes took place at the Seraglio. Relatives of the harem women were summoned to Istanbul to claim their daughters and sisters. Circassian mountaineers and peasants came in droves, clad in the picturesque costume of country folk. They were formally ushered into a large hall of the Seraglio where the ex-Sultan's kadins, concubines, and odalisques came to greet them. The contrast between the elegantly dressed ladies of the palace and the rugged peasant men was dramatic. Everywhere people fell into the arms of their long-unseen loved ones, sobbing uncontrollably. But the most heartbreaking picture was the faces of the women for whom no one came. Kismet left them to the hollow echoes of a dead institution, which, even in their freedom, they could not escape. They remained at the Old Palace, relics of the past, trapped in their liberation. Artists continued immortalizing these beauties with stories of perfumed handkerchiefs, roses, and poems dropped from behind latticed windows.

Benjamin Disraeli

LETTER FROM CONSTANTINOPLE

I CONFESS TO you that my Turkish prejudices are very much confirmed by my residence in Turkey. The life of this people greatly accords with my taste, which is naturally somewhat indolent and melancholy, and I do not think would disgust you. To repose on voluptuous ottomans, and smoke superb pipes, daily to indulge in the luxuries of a bath which requires half a dozen atten-

---

Benjamin Disraeli spent half his time as an English politician and the other half writing historical novel-romances, a number of which starred his friends, Byron and Shelley. In 1830, Parliament business took him to Constantinople, where he scribed this letter.

dants for its perfection, to court the air in a carved caique by shores which are a continual scene and to find no exertion greater than a canter on a barb, is I think a far more sensible life than all the bustle of clubs, and all the boring of saloons—all this without any coloring and exaggeration is the life which may be here commanded accompanied by a thousand sources of calm enjoyment and a thousand modes of mellow pleasure, which it wo[ul]d weary you to relate, and which I leave to your own lively imagination.

I can say nothing about our meeting, but pray that it may be sooner that I can expect. I send you a tobacco bag, that you may sometimes remember me. If ever you have leisure to write me a line, anything directed to *Messrs. Hunter and Ross Malta,* will be forwarded to whatever part of the Levant I may reside in.

I mend slowly, but mend. The seasons have greatly favored me[.] Continual heat, and even here a summer sky, where the winter is proverbially severe.

Remember me most kindly to your brother—and believe me my dear Bulwer

YOURS MOST FAITH[FUL]LY
BENJ. DISRAELI

Simone de Beauvoir

ISTANBUL AT NIGHT

ISTANBUL AT NIGHT looked deserted. Next morning it was teeming with life. Buses, automobiles, handcarts, horse-drawn carriages, bicycles, porters, people walking, the traffic was so thick on the Eminonu bridge that one could scarcely cross the road without risking certain death; all along the wharves, there were clusters of ships: steamships, tugboats, tenders, barges. Their sirens were

French novelist and essayist Simone de Beauvoir is probably best known for her evocative journals and passionate relationship to Jean Paul Sartre. De Beauvoir and Sartre's disconcerting visit to Istanbul is recorded in her 1963 chronicle, Force of Circumstance.

wailing, their engines hiccuping; on the road, overloaded taxis rushed up, skidded, screaming, to a stop, then drove away again in a series of minor explosions; there was the clanging of metal, yells, whistles, a vast discordant uproar reverberating inside our heads already battered by the violent bambardment of the sun. It was like a sledgehammer, yet no reflections spattered the blackish waters of the Golden Horn, cluttered with old tubs and pieces of rotting wood jammed between the warehouses. In the heart of old Stamboul, we clambered up dead streets lined with wooden houses more or less in a state of collapse, and along others with shops and workshops opening off them. Shoeshine boys, cobblers, crouching inside with their gear in front of them, gazed at us with hostility; we got the same looks in the wretched bistro where we drank our coffee at wooden tables; was it Americans they hated, or just tourists? Not a woman in the place; almost none in the streets; nothing but masculine faces, and not one wearing a smile. The covered bazaar, bathed in a flat gray light, made me think of a vast hardware store; everything about the markets in the dusty streets was ugly—the utensils, the stuffs and the cheap pictures. One thing roused our curiosity: the quantity of automatic scales and the number of people, often quite poverty-stricken, who were prepared to sacrifice a coin to weigh themselves. Where were we? These jostling crowds, entirely male, were a sign of the East, of Islam; but the color of Africa and the picturesqueness of China were missing. It felt as though we were on the fringe of a disinherited country, and of some dismal Middle Ages. The interiors of Sancta Sofia and the Blue Mosque lived up to all my expectations; I had seen and liked smaller mosques, more intimate and more alive, with their courtyards, their fountains and pigeons circling overhead; but there was almost nothing left in them of the long-extinguished past. Byzantium, Constantinople, Istanbul: the town did not live up to the promises of these names, except at that hour when its domes and their slender, pointed minarets were silhouetted along the hilltop against the glowing sky at dusk; then all its sumptuous, bloodstained past appeared through its beauty.

We wanted to get to know some Turks. A few weeks earlier, a military *coup d'état* had ousted Mederes; there had been riots in the city with the students joining in: what were they thinking now, what were they doing? Organized tourism has its disadvantages, but our isolation had even more. Annoyed at not being able to get beneath the décor of the place, we left after three days.

Nabi Yousouf Efendi

EULOGY OF CONSTANTINOPLE

O MOON THAT dost light the eye of hope, and dost adorn the days of thy aged father! it availeth thee more to cultivate thy talents than to break the seal of a treasure. Knowledge and instruction have no surer asylum than Constantinople, which has not its equal for the flavor of its intellectual fruit. May God prosper this abode of all greatness, the home and school of all great

Nabi Yousouf Efendi's stories and poetry, which date from the late 1600s, have earned him a top spot in Turkish literature. Efendi resided in Constantinople, where he worked as president of the State treasury and comptroller of the cavalry.

men, and the seat of administration for all people!
There merit always finds consideration. Every perfection, every talent, is there esteemed at its just value.
There are all the degrees of honor and of nobility;
everywhere else life is lost and wasted. There everything
has its peaceable course, and merit has not the injustice
of fortune to fear. There are found all places, all dignities, and all careers. Heaven in vain revolves around the
world, it sees nowhere a city like unto Constantinople.
There are seen paintings, drawings, writings, and gild-
ings, dazzling and gleaming beyond belief. All possible
kinds of arts contribute their own brilliancy and splendor. See how she gleams with a beauty all her own, as
the sea languidly caresses her!

At Constantinople all arts and all professions
are esteemed and honored, and one finds here talents
whose names even are unknown elsewhere. Does he who
is outside the house know what is within? Does he who
stands on the shore see what is hidden by the depth of

the sea? There also they excel in archery and the names of conquerors are immortalized on stone. Without mention of the rest, how pleasant and charming it is to fly over the surface of the sea, to reign at the same time over the air and the waves, like Solomon in his throne, and to recline luxuriously on a cushion with eyes fixed on a mirror of silver! There are combined at once music, song, and all pleasures. There, riding on the wings of the wind, the eyes perceive a great number of cities. Tranquilly resting on the breeze, one traverses the earth without fatigue. There are marvellously reflected the most gorgeous spectacles, which seem to mirror one another and give an enchanted aspect to the shores. The *quaîqs* glide lightly over the water, with their wind-filled sails like a bird's wings. How can so beautiful a sight be described? what need has it of eulogy?

Behold Saint Sophia, marvel of the world, whose cupola might be termed the eighth celestial body. Nowhere has she her equal, save, perhaps in paradise.

Contemplate the imperial seat of the sultans of the world, the dwelling of the kings of time, the court of the Ottoman Empire, and the centre of the rule of the khans. In this ever-blessed region is found all that is desirable. Whatever thou canst imagine, she possesses in the highest degree. She combines the elect of the beys, of the pachas, and the efendis, the most illustrious warriors and the most renowned wise men.

All the world's difficulties there find their solutions: all efforts are there crowned with success. The mind cannot conceive all the charms she contains. If she were not afflicted with all kinds of disease and the abominable plague, who would consent to leave this celestial abode whence care is forever exiled? If her temperature were more equal, would she not cause the rest of the world to be forgotten? Whoever has an established fortune should not establish his home in any other country. No city, no country, resembles or is comparable to her. She is the asylum of all sciences:

everywhere else study is neglected for gain, commerce, agriculture, or usury, so that all vestiges of knowledge have disappeared. Money takes the place of talent in a province, and it seems as if merit could be extracted from it. In the provinces scientific men have become extinct and books are forgotten. Poetry and prose are both held in aversion, and even a Persian phrase is tabooed. The study of Arabic has vanished as snow without consistency, and the principles of grammar and syntax are entirely neglected. Luxury and presumption have intoxicated all hearts, and there is no worship but that of dignities and employments. There one finds neither virtue nor knowledge, and morality is outraged.

The ambition to secure vain honors leaves no time for the labor for perfection. How many do not lift up their voices unto the Lord except when their fortunes are threatened by reverses! It is by a special dispensation of Providence that God has withdrawn learning from the provinces. If he had not first chained them in ignorance, who could have governed such men? The seat of power belongs to the great, but pride is the part of provincials. He who is high placed is not vain-glorious; but these wretches are filled with arrogance. The constantly compare their dignity and importance to that of the representatives of authority.

But what would it be if they possessed learning? They would not deign to look at their fellows. They know not their value, and take no account of their worth.

Nothing teaches the inferiority of the provinces more than the sight of Constantinople. In the gatherings of the capital he who passes elsewhere for a wisest man of the century is but a blockhead; the strong-minded loses his assurance, and the fine talker has no longer a tongue. They who boasted so loudly of their rank and nobility are only admitted to the most commonplace circles. The arrogant, who knit his brows so disdain-fully, eagerly seeks the door-keepers. He who bore a title so pompously cannot even obtain the honor of kissing the hem of a robe. He who occupied the first place is not even deemed worthy to remain at the door. What city can be compared to Constantinople? Is not the prince above him whose homage he receives? After the capital, there is no place so charming as Halep. Halep! honor of the province, illustrious and flourishing city; the resort of Indians, Europeans, and Chinese; object of the envy of the whole universe; the market of all merchandise; haven of joys and wealth, with thy delicious waters and climate, thy vast plains and magnificent buildings.

J. F. Packard

ULYSSES S. GRANT IN CONSTANTINOPLE

THE NEXT POINT visited by the travellers was Constantinople. The steamer rounded the Seraglio Point, and sweeping into the bold expanse which the Bosphorus forms opposite the city, dropped anchor off the mouth of the Golden Horn. The first step upon the shore reminds one that he is in the East. The costume is oriental, the language has nothing in

J. F. Packard was the official historian for Ulysses S. Grant's "Grand Tour Around the World" in 1880. The president and his entourage bounded through Britain, Europe, North Africa and the Far East in the 1870s; Packard supplied the commentary.

its syllables or sounds that resemble the provençal tongues, and there appears to be an air of luxurious enjoyment and repose in all around, that contrasts strikingly with the anxious air of the busy populations of the cities of Western Europe.

Almost touching the water was a café, cooled by a fountain, and the umbrageous boughs of the wide-spreading *platanus* tree. Lounging on divans were a number of Turks, with white turbans and long beards, smoking the nargile, or water-pipe, and seeking nervous excitement in frequents draughts of coffee, or in the inhalation of the intoxicating fumes of hashish. Near by was a beautiful fountain, erected by some Turk who was seeking entrance into the Mussulman heaven by doing good to man, and a mosque from the minarets of which the muezzin was calling the faithful to prayer. "There is no god but God, and Mohammed is His prophet," was the cry that was floating on the air as the travellers landed.

The interior of Constantinople by no means corresponds with the expectations which one is led to entertain from the splendor of its appearance as seen from the Bosphorus. The streets are narrow, and paved with stones which appear as though they had been scattered at random, simply to cover the nakedness of the earth. The houses are of wood, and so wretchedly built, that they afford but little shelter against the elements. Fires at Constantinople, where the buildings are of frame, are, of course, very destructive, sometimes sweeping away squares of houses at a time. There are two lofty towers which overlook the city, where the watchmen are stationed night and day to sound the alarm of fire; but a conflagration rarely breaks out which does not destroy a square of buildings. The Turks will sometimes make an effort to arrest the flames, but if overmastered, they will quietly fold their arms, and exclaiming *"Allah kerim,"* "God is great," leave things to take their course.

After sunset, the city is enveloped in darkness, as there is not a single lamp in the streets to lighten the path of the wanderer with the glimmer of a friendly ray. If you do not wish to be devoured alive by the troops of savage dogs which infest the streets, you must carry a lantern; and if your light should happen to go out, you must make the best of it. A distinguished traveller says:—"For myself, in a desperate battle which I had with some canine ruffians, in passing through one of the cemeteries late at night, my light was not only extinguished, but being overpowered by fearful odds, I was obliged to take to my heels, priding myself more on my chances to escape from their fangs than upon the glory of vanquishing my foes."

The channel of the Golden Horn, which comes in from the Bosphorus, divides Constantinople in two parts. On the west site is Stamboul, Constantinople *proper,* where the Turks reside, and where the principal bazaars are. On the east side are the suburbs of Galata and Pera. Galata lies at the foot of the hill, and is the port to which all Frank vessels resort. It is the residence chiefly of Greeks, while higher up the hill you pass a kind of neutral ground, occupied by the bankers and large merchants of all nations; and continuing your walk higher up, you enter the precincts of Pera, which contains the private residences of the Frank merchants, and the offices of the European ambassadors. Most of the foreign ministers, however, live on the shores of the Bosphorus, at Therapia, or in the surrounding country, only resorting to Pera a few hours during the day. The hill is occupied with buildings from the water's edge to the summit, and it is somewhat puzzling to know where Galata ends or Pera begins.

When General Grant reached Constantinople his first visit was paid to the Sultan, who immediately ordered Munir Bey, the Master of Ceremonies, to present the General an Arab horse from the imperial stables. One was chosen and set aside for him, but, owing to some misunderstanding, the gift horse was not sent, and the Vandalia sailed without him. Afterwards, the question having been revived, the steed in question was hunted up among the 570 horses which composed the imperial stud. He was found, and, accompanied by a second horse, transferred to the care of the officers of the American Legation, by whom they were shipped on board the Norman Monarch. They were housed between the decks, provided with canvas belts to swing in in rough weather, and in every way treated as cabin passengers, a man being detailed to care for them. They are said to have endured the long voyage without showing any signs of discomfort or fatigue, and were described by one of the prominent horsemen at Suffolk Park as being in perfect trim and models of beauty. They are in many respects unlike the blooded American horse. They are about fifteen hands in height, and of a graceful and well-rounded, though wiry and strong, figure. Both the animals are of a beautiful dapple-gray color, with a soft skin and shiny coat. Their manes and tails are of a dark color and very long. A wide difference from the average European or American animals is said to be discernible in every feature, and the eye, ear, and nostril are indicative of some particular quality, such as shrewdness, quickness, and wonderful intelligence. The neck is arched and the head is held very high.

These beautiful creatures were consigned to the care of George W. Childs, Esq., of Philadelphia, who at once caused the old shoes to be removed and new ones put on. The shoes taken from their feet were very thin plates of iron, without corks of any kind. They covered all parts of the hoof except the frog. A circular hole was pierced for that. These specimens of Turkish handi-craft were carefully preserved upon being removed, and will eventually appear on the walls of General Grant's billiard-room. They are to be brightened and decorated in fine style. One of them was given to Mr. Bishop, of the firm of horse-shoers. He refused $6 for it. It is said that $5 were offered for one of the shoe-nails. The horses' feet had to be trimmed. This as well as the subsequent shoeing was done under the supervision of a veterinary doctor. The shoes were very light ones, made particularly for the purpose.

General Grant has also placed all the presents which he received while abroad under the care of Mr. Childs. They were for a time on exhibition in Memorial Hall, Fairmount Park, Philadelphia. There they proved one of the most attractive centres of interest and were visited by thousands of people. The gifts consist of twenty-four engrossed and illuminated scrolls, albums and portfolios, containing addresses of welcome from working-men and corporations, the freedom of cities and other expressions of esteem for General Grant. Some are in gold and some in silver caskets of very rich workmanship. In some instances the seals also are enclosed in gold cases. One of the most interesting souvenirs is a beautifully carved box made of mulberry wood from the tree at Stratford-on-Avon, planted by Shakespeare, and presented to General Grant by the corporation of the town.

One of the most interesting places in Constantinople is the Slave-Market. To this no Frank is allowed to enter without an authorized janissary of one of the embassies. The visitor upon entering is at once saluted with "Backshish! Backshish!" The area of the square was filled with groups of Nubian and Abyssinian slaves, mostly children, and in a state of almost perfect nudity. They were crouched together in groups, but seemed to be by no means disconsolate at their lot. They were cheerful and full of merriment. Around the court-yard, under the sheds, were compartments for the better order of slaves. These were chiefly African women. We saw only two white female slaves, and these were Georgians, destined for the harems of the rich. We were very solicitous to get a look at these Georgian beauties, but were only indulged with a glance through the bars of their cages. We saw only the bright black eyes of these imprisoned ones; they were merry enough.

The slave-merchants were quietly reposing on carpets under the sheds, smoking, and answering with usual Turkish *nonchalance* the propositions of customers. Their stoical indifference to the condition of the slaves, and the manner in which they handled and spoke of them as mere merchandise, disgusted us, and we were glad to leave the place where humanity sinks to the level of the brute creation.

Our next visit was to the bazaars. These consist of a long range of shops running parallel with each other, with an intervening paved avenue dividing the two rows; the avenue is covered over. There are numerous bazaars, each division being appropriated to the sale of different objects. There is the silk bazaar, the provision bazaar, the arm bazaar, etc. The purchaser is not, therefore, obliged to wander through the whole range of bazaars to seek the object of his wants, but at once goes to a particular bazaar and finds it. The shops are very small, and contain but scanty stocks; but there is a great number of them, which may, in some degree, compensate for the lack of quantity in their stock.

The next point visited was the Mosque of the Sultan Ahmed. The exterior walls of this, as the walls of all other mosques, are painted white. From the centre rises a hemispherical dome, and at the four corners of the building shoot up tall minarets, the points of which, tipped with gold, appear lost in the air. Passing through an open court-yard, we came to the portal of the mosque. We pulled off our boots, slid our feet into yellow slippers, the color worn only by the faithful, removed our hats, and entered. The interior was very plain; the floor was spread with rich carpets, and variously-colored glass lamps, like those in public gardens, were suspended around the walls, with here and there an ostrich-egg, the offering of some pious devotee. A pulpit of carved wood faced the east. Several

Turks were prostrating themselves in prayer upon the carpets, the countenance turned to the sacred east. From the floor to the ceiling the breadth and width of the great space beneath the roof was unbroken by a gallery or any other object. The roof rested upon arches which sprang from the walls. This great void, with the overhanging roof unsustained by a single pillar, had a most majestic effect, and I have rarely seen boldness and simplicity of architecture so happily combined as in this mosque. The walls were naked of ornaments, with the exception of a rude drawing of the Caaba at Mecca.

In the centre of the court-yard of the mosque was a beautiful fountain, ornamented with that light tracery work which is characteristic of Saracenic architecture. An immense number of pigeons had assembled there at that time to be fed, as some kind Mussulman had left a legacy to procure grain for the daily feeding of the pigeons which belonged to the mosque. They nearly covered the yard, and children were walking about in the midst of them, without causing them the least alarm. Such is the friendship between man and the brute creation in Mussulman countries.

Gore Vidal

AUGUSTUS

ON 11 DECEMBER 361 I entered Constantinople as Roman Emperor. Snow fell at slow intervals and the great flakes turned like feathers in air so still that the day was almost warm. The sky was low and the color of tarnished silver. There was no color that day in nature, only in man, but what color! It was a day of splendor.

Novelist and essayist Gore Vidal is best known for his regular, barbarous attacks on political corruption. He is also the author of several novels, including Myra Breckinridge, Lincoln *and* Golgotha. *"Augustus" is from the 1964 novel of the Roman Empire,* Julian.

In front of the Golden Gate, close to the sea of Marmora, the Scholarians in full-dress uniform stood at attention. On each of the brick towers at either side of the gate, the dragons were unfurled. The green bronze gates were shut. As custom demanded, I dismounted a few yards from the wall. The commander of the Scholarians gave me a silver hammer. With it I struck the bronze gate three times. From within, came the voice of the city's prefect. "Who goes there?"

"Julian Augustus," I replied in a loud voice. "A citizen of the city."

"Enter Julian Augustus."

The bronze gates swung open noiselessly and there before me in the inner courtyard stood the prefect of the city—and some two thousand men of senatorial rank. The Sacred Consistory was also there, having preceded me into the capital the night before. Quite alone, I passed through the gate and took possession of the City of Constantine.

Trumpets sounded. The people cheered. I was particularly struck by the brightness of the clothes they wore. I don't know whether it was the white setting which made the reds and greens, the yellows and blues almost unbearably vivid, or the fact that I had been away too long in northern countries where all colors are as muted and as dim as the forests in which the people live. But this was not the misty north. This was Constantinople, and despite the legend that we are the New Rome (and like that republican city, austere, stern, virtuous), we are not Rome at all. We are Asia. I thought of this as I was helped into the gold chariot of Constantine, recalling with amusement Eutherius's constant complaint, "You are hopelessly Asiatic!" Well, I am Asiatic! And I was home at last.

As flakes of snow settled in my hair and beard, I rode down Middle Street. Everywhere I looked I saw changes. The city had altered completely in the few years I had been away. For one thing, it has outgrown the wall of Constantine. What were once open fields are now crowded suburbs, and one day I shall have to go to the expense of building a new wall to contain these suburbs, which, incidentally, are not carefully laid out in the way the city was but simply created helter-skelter by contractors interested only in a quick profit.

Colonnades line Middle Street from one end to the other. The arcades were crowded with people who cheered me ecstatically. Why? Because they loved me? No. Because I was a novelty. The people tire of the same ruler, no matter how excellent. They had got bored with Constantius and they wanted a change of program and I was it.

Suddenly I heard what sounded like thunder at my back. For a moment I took it as an omen that Zeus had approved me. Then I realized it was not thunder but my army singing the marching song of Julius Caesar's troops: *"Ecce Caesar nunc triumphat, Qui subegit Gallias!"* It is the sound of war itself, and of all earthly glory.

The prefect of the city walked beside my chariot and tried to point out the new buildings, but I could not hear him for the noise of the mob. Even so, it was exhilarating to see so much activity, in contrast to old cities like Athens and Milan where a new building is a rarity. When an old house collapses in Athens, the occupants simply move into another one, for there are far more houses than people. But everything in Constantinople is brand-new, including the population, which is now—the prefect shouted to me just as we entered the Forum of Constantine—close to a million people, counting slaves and foreigners.

The colossal statue of Constantine at the center of the oval forum always gives me a shock. I can never get used to it. On a tall column of porphyry, my uncle set up a statue of Apollo, stolen I believe from Delos. He then knocked the head off this masterpiece and substituted his own likeness, an inferior piece of work by any standard and so badly joined that there is a dark ring where head and neck meet. The people refer to this monument as "old dirty neck." On the head there is a monstrous halo of seven bronze rays, perfect blasphemy, not only to the true gods but to the Galilean as well. Constantine saw himself as both Galilean and as incarnation of the sun god. He was most ambitious. I am told he doted on this particular statue and used to look at it every chance he got; he even pretended that the Apollonian body was his own!

We then entered that section of Middle Street which is called Imperial Way and leads into the Augusteum, a large porticoed square which was the center of the city when it was called Byzantium. In the middle of the Augusteum, Constantine set up a large statue of his mother Helena. She is seated on a throne and looks quite severe; in one hand she holds a piece of wood said to have been a part of the cross to which the Galilean was nailed. My great-aunt had a passion for relics; she was also infinitely gullible. There is not a charnel house in the city to which she did not give some sliver of wood, shred of cloth, bit of bone said to have been associated in one way or another with that unfortunate rabbi and his family.

To my astonishment, the entire north side of the square was taken up by the basilica of a charnel house so new that the scaffolding had not yet been removed from the front. The prefect beamed cheerfully at me, thinking I would be pleased.

"Augustus may recall the old church that was here? the small one the Great Constantine dedicated to Holy Wisdom? Well, the Emperor Constantius has had it enlarged. In fact, only last summer he rededicated it."

I said nothing but immediately vowed to turn Saint Sophia into a temple to Athena. It would never do to have a Galilean monument right at my front door (the main entrance to the palace is on the south side of the square, just opposite the charnel house). To the east is the senate house to which the senators were now repairing. The senate's usual quorum is fifty, but today all two thousand were present, elbowing one another as they hurried up the slippery steps.

The square was now jammed with people, and no one knew what to do next. The prefect was used to being given his orders by the palace chamberlains, who were, if nothing else, masters of pageantry. But today the chamberlains were in hiding and neither the prefect nor I knew what to do. I'm afraid between us we made rather a botch of things.

My chariot had stopped at the Milion, a covered monument from which all distances in the empire are measured. Yes, we counterfeit Rome in this, too; in everything, even to the seven hills.

"The senate waits for you, Lord," said the prefect nervously.

"*Waits* for me? They're still trying to get inside the senate house!"

"Perhaps the Augustus would prefer to receive them in the palace?"

I shook my head, vowing that never again would I enter a city without preparation. No one knew where to go or what to do. I saw several of my commanders arguing with the Scholarians, who did not know them, while ancient senators slipped and fell in the slush. It was a mess, and a bad omen. Already I was handling matters less well than Constantius.

I pulled myself together. "Prefect, while the senate meets, I shall make sacrifice."

The prefect indicated Saint Sophia. "The bishop should be inside, Augustus. If he's not, I can send for him."

"Sacrifice to the true gods," I said firmly.

"But . . . *where?*" The poor man was bewildered, with good reason. After all, Constantinople is a new city, dedicated to Jesus, and there are no temples except for three small ones on the old Byzantine acropolis. They would have to do. I motioned to those members of my entourage who had got through the guards and together we made a small ragged procession to the low hills where stood the shabby and deserted temples of Apollo, Artemis and Aphrodite.

In the dank filthy temple of Apollo, I gave thanks to Helios and to all the gods, while the townspeople crowded round outside, amused by this first show of imperial eccentricity. As I sacrificed, I swore to Apollo that I would rebuild his temple.

Nazim Hikmet

ISTANBUL HOUSE OF DETENTION

IN THE ISTANBUL Detention House yard
on a sunny winter day after rain,
as clouds, red tiles, walls, and my face
       trembled in the puddles on the ground,
I—with what was bravest and meanest in me,
what was strongest and weakest—
I thought of the world, my country, and you.

Nazim Hikmet is considered Turkey's greatest modern poet. His controversial themes landed him in Turkish jails for over 18 years; Hikmet spent the last decade of his life in exile, where he died in 1963. "Istanbul House of Detention" is from the new collection, Poems of Nazim Hikmet.

My love,
they're on the march:
heads forward, eyes wide open,
the red glare of burning cities,
               crops trampled,
             endless
                     footsteps.
And people slaughtered:
       like trees and calves,
      only easier
           and faster.

My love,
amid these footsteps and this slaughter
I sometimes lost my freedom, bread, and you,
but never my faith in the days that will come
out of the darkness, screams, and hunger
to knock on our door with hands full of sun.

I'm wonderfully happy I came into the world:
I love its earth, light, struggle, bread.
Although I know its dimension from pole to pole
                    to the centimeter,
and while I'm not unaware it's a mere toy next to the sun,
the world for me is unbelievably big.
I would have liked to go around the world
and see the fish, fruits, and stars I haven't seen.
However,
I made my European trip only in books and pictures.
In my whole life I never got one letter
          with its blue stamp canceled in Asia.
Me and our corner grocer,
we're both mightily unknown in America.
Nevertheless,
from China to Spain, from the Cape of Good Hope to Alaska,
in every nautical mile, in every kilometer, I have friends
                    and enemies.
Such friends that we haven't met even once

yet we can die for the same bread, the same freedom, the same
   dream.
And such enemies that they thirst for my blood—
                I thirst for theirs.
My strength
is that I'm not alone in this big world.
The world and its people are no secret in my heart,
              no mystery in my science.
Calmly and openly
     I took my place
          in the great struggle.
And without it,
     you and the earth
          are not enough for me.
And yet you are astonishingly beautiful,
        the earth is warm and beautiful.

I love my country:
I've swung on its plane trees,

I've slept in its prisons.
Nothing lifts my spirits like its songs and tobacco.

My country:
Bedreddin, Sinan, Yunus Emré, and Sakarya,
lead domes and factory chimneys—
it's all the work of my people, whose drooping mustaches
hide their smiles
even from themselves.

My country:
so big
it seems endless.
Edirné, Izmir, Ulukishla, Marash, Trabzon, Erzurum.
All I know of the Erzurum plateau are its songs,
and I'm ashamed to say
I never crossed the Tauruses
to visit the cotton pickers
                in the south.

My country:
camels, trains, Fords, and sick donkeys,
poplars
　　　　willow trees,
　　　　　　　and red earth.

My country:
goats on the Ankara plain,
the sheen of their long blond silky hair.
The succulent plump hazelnuts of Giresun.
Amasya apples with fragrant red cheeks,
olives,
　　　　figs,
　　　　　　　melons,
and bunches and bunches of grapes
　　　　　　　　　　all colors,
then plows
and black oxen
and then my people,

ready to embrace
>with the wide-eyed joy of children
anything modern, beautiful, and good—
my honest, hard-working, brave people,
>half full, half hungry,

>>half slaves. . .

Acknowledgments

"Song of a Dweller in a High-Rise Block" by Gülten Akin ©1992 by Ruth Christie. Reprinted by permission of The Rockingham Press.

"Istanbul at Night" from *Force of Circumstance* by Simone de Beauvoir ©1963 by Librairie Gallimard. Reprinted by permission of Editions Gallimard.

"Flight from Byzantium" by Joseph Brodsky ©1985 by Joseph Brodsky. Reprinted by permission of Farrar, Straus & Giroux, Inc.

Excerpt from *Harem* by Alev Lytle Croutier ©1989 Alev Lytle Croutier. Reprinted by permission of Abbeville Press.

"The Lords and Ladies of Byzantium" from *Turkish Reflections* by Mary Lee Settle ©1991 by Mary Lee Settle. Reprinted by permission of Simon & Schuster, Inc.

"Istanbul" from *Pole to Pole* by Michael Palin ©1992 by Michael Palin. Reprinted by permission of BBC Books.

"Julian" from *Augustus* by Gore Vidal ©1962 by Gore Vidal. Reprinted by permission of Little, Brown & Company.

"Istanbul House of Detention" from *Poems of Nazim Hikmet* by Nazim Hikmet, translated by Randy Blasing and Mutlu Knouk, ©1994 by Randy Blasing and Mutlu Knouk. Reprinted by permission of Persea Books.